The Birds of Opulence

The
Birds of
Opulence

Crystal Wilkinson

UNIVERSITY PRESS OF KENTUCKY

Scholarly publisher for the Commonwealth,
serving Bellarmine University, Berea College, Centre
College of Kentucky, Eastern Kentucky University,
The Filson Historical Society, Georgetown College,
Kentucky Historical Society, Kentucky State University,
Morehead State University, Murray State University,
Northern Kentucky University, Transylvania University,
University of Kentucky, University of Louisville,
and Western Kentucky University.
All rights reserved.

Editorial and Sales Offices: The University Press of Kentucky
663 South Limestone Street, Lexington, Kentucky 40508-4008
www.kentuckypress.com

Library of Congress Cataloging-in-Publication Data

Names: Wilkinson, Crystal, author.
Title: The birds of Opulence / Crystal Wilkinson.
Description: Lexington, Kentucky : The University Press of Kentucky,
    [2016]
Identifiers: LCCN 2015041245| ISBN 9780813166919 (hardcover : acid-
    free paper) | ISBN 9780813166933 (pdf) | ISBN 9780813166926 (epub)
Subjects: LCSH: African American families—Fiction. | City and town
    life—Fiction. | Domestic fiction.
Classification: LCC PS3573.I44184 B57 2016 | DDC 813/.54—dc23 LC
    record available at http://lccn.loc.gov/2015041245

This book is printed on acid-free paper meeting
the requirements of the American National Standard
for Permanence in Paper for Printed Library Materials.

Manufactured in the United States of America.

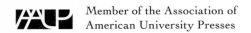 Member of the Association of
American University Presses

For Christine, Dorsie, and Lovester
(the holy trinity of mothers)

Contents

Contents

1962

The Known Bird.

Yolanda

Imagine a tree, a bird in the tree, the hills, the creek, a possum, the dog chasing the possum. Imagine yourself a woman who gathers stories in her apron.

The sun peeped through the silver maples the day I was born. In the back field, one of Old Man Lucien's beagles cornered a possum. The dog snarled, pulled back on her haunches, and bit the possum's neck and hindquarters. The possum, bloody and scared, caught in the first streams of daylight, played dead. Up on the knob, mist burned off quickly into another hot day.

Outside, my daddy, Joe Brown, tinkered underneath the hood of his pickup. Scars webbed out like a map on his hands, the longest one disappearing between the thumb and forefinger of his right hand. The smell of coffee drifted from the house into the driveway. He looked back toward the porch, where the kitchen was, and knew my mother would be calling him to the table soon. He sped up his work, quickened his hands.

Sometimes a discomfort settles in Daddy's back. He stops whatever he's doing, holds his palms to his kidneys, and says "Mercy!" A look of longing slides down his face. We can see he misses Aunt Jo and Uncle Peck, who took him in as a boy when his mother died and raised him in the city. But he'd been away from them for more than twenty years by the time I was born. By then, Daddy was devoted to Mama, devoted to all of us. He had already learned how to blend into this river of crazy women.

On that day, by the time he moved from the pickup to the Plymouth, morning had opened like an orange flower. He smeared grease on his forehead when he reached to wipe the sweat. Later, he would change the oil on Clem Jenkins's Ford and replace a muffler on Mrs. Carter's Oldsmobile.

Inside the house, Mama Minnie, my great-grandmother, rubbed the low swell of my mother's belly. I was there, quiet as a bird, curled like a question mark, waiting. Mama Minnie thumped Mama's belly as if it were a melon, then pushed gently, pressure I could feel from inside.

"She's a good size," Mama Minnie said to all her girls: Mama, Granny Tookie, and even me.

"*She*?" Mama asked.

"Yes, *she*!"

Tookie, my grandmother, swept the floor and sucked her teeth and bounced the dirt off the broom hard when she heard Mama Minnie say I was a girl. She checked the biscuits, turned the bacon with a fork, winced at the heat; she felt a headache coming on.

"Lucy, sure as I'm Minnie Mae Goode, that's a girl in there."

Mama Minnie patted Mama's belly again, then poured the last bit of raw egg from the bowl into the hot skillet.

Mama pulled dishes from the cabinet, sat five plates on the table.

Mama Minnie groaned, sort of sung.

Tookie made a clicking noise in her throat, adding to the rhythm.

My brother, Kevin, who we've always called Kee Kee, played under the kitchen table. If he craned his neck toward the ceiling he could see their faces, but he already knew the expressions they were making. He watched their feet moving from one side of the green linoleum to the other. He knew their kitchen dance well. He pushed a car along the floor, letting it crash into the table leg. A growl grew louder in his stomach and blended with the scraping, the humming, the scooting sounds of his family. He watched Mama Minnie, Granny Tookie, and Mama, already learning the ways of women.

Mama poured coffee.

Mama Minnie pulled out a stick of butter.

Granny Tookie stirred a pan of sweet rice, and couldn't stop herself from thinking her new grandchild should be another boy. *Boy give you less to worry about.*

But Mama Minnie was sure of the signs when she saw a bird on the window ledge—not a Kentucky bird that she could identify: a rare bird with a breast of red, freckled with yellow dots. She sunk the heavy skillet into the hot water, its weight straining against her wrist. The bird perched on a branch outside the window and ruffled its feathers, then pranced in a full circle before it looked Mama Minnie square in the face and cocked its pretty head like it was listening to what she had to say.

"Won't be long," she whispered to the listening bird and to herself.

This knowing, reading signs, was as familiar as her own two hands.

A long time ago, when Mama Minnie was a girl, women down home came to *her* mama's kitchen door looking to know what sign of the moon to cut a baby's hair, when to wean it from its mother's nipple, whether the ball of woman's belly contained girl or boy. Even the white women came with their full bellies and colicky babies.

Now Mama Minnie was the one who could spot a woman in the family way, before anyone else, sometimes even before the mother knew herself. Had nothing to do with the belly, had to do with "that look around the eyes" when they were baby-full, she'd say. She delivered babies too, though women don't catch babies for one another much anymore. They go to the hospital.

"Seen more tail than most men," she said. "Saw just about every woman from Opulence to Dry Ridge, on up across Patsy Rife, and clear on up to the Tennessee border with their legs spread. Sweating, gripping a bed sheet, bringing along another life to this old suffering world."

And of course she could gauge the weight of a reaching child on a woman's hip, squeezing sweet fat knees around a mama's waist. Twelve pounds, fifteen, eight. If it was a scrawny baby, she'd look the mother right in the eyes and say, "Feed that baby some sugar rice."

"Nothing like a young un in this whole world," she said.

She had given birth to three round-faced babies of her own. First Uncle Butter, then Uncle June, then Granny Tookie, who never left home until the day she died, unlike the boys.

Outside, Hazel Sloan came out on her porch, shook her rugs into the yard, and greeted my father.

A dog barked down the road somewhere.

Daddy glanced up from the hood, nodded his head, threw up his hand.

He looked up at the hills. That astronaut, John Glenn, had gone clean around the world in four hours. Daddy wondered what it felt like to be that high up. He looked up at the trees, to the hazy sky, and then again to the hills. The look of those hills come morning—the fog rising up like God's hand on them—always amazed him. In fact, he was amazed at everything he saw outdoors. Sometimes he'd walk to the edge of town to see the hills better, or drive down to the homeplace before dawn just to watch the sunrise over the pines while the dew was still in.

He had never thought he'd become a country man, but by then it was too late.

Daddy's buddies back in the city would get a big laugh if they could see him out hoeing a garden, working on a car in an open field, standing with a walking stick, looking down on a meadow.

"Joe Brown's a country nigger now," they'd say.

Mama hollered out the side porch door. She waved him inside.

Hazel Sloan was watering her plants; so many plants that she would still be pouring water from her jug when we were half through with breakfast. Miss Hazel turned to wave at Mama, pausing to stand straight up.

"You sure poking out there."

Hazel made a round motion in front of her own waist.

"Eight months along," said Mama. She cocked her head like that listening bird, patted the place where I waited, and slipped back inside our house.

The heat was beginning to come on quick, but it was not quite hot yet. A snake slithered through the grass and into the blackness of a garage. Old Man Lucien's beagle had left the possum for dead, but returned now to find the possum gone, the scent lost.

Later, after Sunday school, even though Mama Minnie thought it was too much toil on the Lord's Day, we headed to the garden.

My brother ran circles, roaring like an airplane, the quilt draped over his shoulders flapping in the wind like a flying thing. I was still inside Mama's belly, but I could also fly out and around, watching all of this before I was born. Granny Tookie grinned at Kee Kee, but lost her smile just as quick once the Plymouth was in motion and there was nothing to do but drive and think. It was the thinking that was bothersome to her. Memory reached out, swirled around her head, and pounded like a fist. A headache pressed at her temples.

Mama poked near her navel, right where I strained her womb. I wonder if she loved me then. I moved a foot or an arm from time to time, just to let her know I was there, waiting. I stretched myself out along her ribs. My spirit stretched itself out and flew around in the sky a time or two before settling back inside her.

Granny Tookie pulled the Plymouth off the gravel road and down the path to the garden.

Kee Kee pulled candy from a sack and jingled the pennies in his pocket. He rolled out of the backseat, followed by a round, staggering Mama. He ran his finger through the dust that coated the car, and popped his finger into his mouth before Mama could stop him.

Mama Minnie rose up from the front passenger's seat and steadied herself with her cane. She closed her eyes and prayed. Granny Tookie had already opened the trunk and removed the metal buckets before Mama Minnie opened her eyes again.

"Let's get a move on, make this quick."

Granny's eyes centered on my mama's protruding navel like a bull's-eye.

Trees formed a curtain around the holler and danced in the whiteness of afternoon sunlight. The smokehouse sat next to the garden. A rusting tub, wire, and sweetgrass string hung on the outside of the building. In the center of the yard, a well support leaned; the water dipper, secured by a nail and chain, still gleamed with flecks of silver through the rust. The old house loomed in the distance, its gray shingle siding glistening in the sun.

All was old and good here at the homeplace, and we could all feel something shifting.

A feeling seeped into Mama Minnie's bones, a feeling like the return of everything lost. Old-time people from across the waters gathered all around her. She put her bony hand on her hip. Every yesterday converged.

A pair of crows cawed from the apple tree, and a squirrel scampered through the underbrush. Kee Kee looked for it, pulling back the branches and weeds. He turned to Granny Tookie for help, but she was looking up toward the top of the trees. He turned his head, hoping she had spotted a hawk, but there was nothing there he could see but sky.

Granny thumped her chest, cleared her throat. Ma Teke's black walnut pie and apple dumplings; playing tag with Tess and Lou Lou around the holly bush; Pa Green whittling her a play-pretty from a piece of firewood; the grand whisper of daffodils in spring. Granny was running with plaits splayed out around her shoulders, her bangs sticking straight out stiff as a pinecone. Over the hill, behind the smokehouse, brown legs skipped all around. Then girlish frolic halted, entombed somewhere deep within the walls of Granny Tookie's chest. She put her hands to her throat and coughed hard, but nothing came up.

"You alright, Mama?" my mother asked.

"Must be these weeds."

Mama grabbed one of the buckets and reached low to the

ground to snap the squash from the vines. It was, as it had been for some time, hard to work around me, like having an extra appendage. Blood rushed to her cheeks. A tendril of hair coiled up like a grapevine and fell into her face. She grunted each time she bent. When she fetched another squash, Kee Kee crooked toward the ground with her. He pulled milk thistle, Queen Anne's lace, and pokeweed. The legs of his pants were already covered in cockleburs. He scratched at his ankles.

Mama Minnie and Granny picked, their buckets filling more quickly than Mama's.

"Boy, watch out for snakes," Granny said to Kee Kee.

I settled my head against a pillow above my mother's tailbone.

Mama stretched up one way then down the other. She was hot. The chiggers were biting her ankles. She tugged at the front of her dress and tried to move me to a more comfortable spot with her fingertips. She looked around, and her mind set on a shady spot underneath the apple tree. The outhouse seemed miles away. Her legs grew wobbly, like two thin branches. The raw smell of freshly turned dirt churned her stomach, made her head swim.

Mama Minnie and Granny moved over the potato vines, turning each of the leaves to make sure the bugs weren't eating them up.

"Too hot, Lucy?"

Mama Minnie had one eye on Mama's sweaty face, one on that place that held me.

"Do nicely with a pot of green beans," Granny Tookie said, shaking dirt clods free from a handful of new potatoes.

Mama Minnie nodded, glanced toward Mama again.

Kee Kee stepped carefully through the garden, so as not to land his foot on a squash. When he was one giant step away from her, a stream of water trickled down our mother's leg.

Mama stood in the squash patch, her back humped over, and the wet spot grew wider in the dirt beneath her.

Mama Minnie sent Kee Kee for the quilt from the car.

Granny watched a buzzard soaring low up over the hills.

Kee Kee ran toward them with the quilt, shaking out candy wrappers and pennies.

Mama Minnie anchored her walking stick in the dirt and spread the quilt on the ground.

"What's Mama doing?"

"Hush boy," Granny said, and patted Kee Kee on the head as she squatted beside Mama.

"Is Mama going to die?"

"Go on, now, back to picking your weeds." Her voice was sugar, was biscuit-warm. "Go on," she said again.

But Kee Kee stayed, watched, even when he didn't want to. Mama Minnie squatted. My grandmother kneeled. Mama thrashed around on the quilt, flopped on her back. Her legs and arms were like spinning wheels.

"Scat on, boy," my Granny Tookie said. "Ain't nothing here for you to see."

But Kee Kee watched. He watched Mama balance on her elbows and knees with her head down low to the ground. He watched Mama Minnie and Granny Tookie bare Mama's private place, and as the day wore on he eventually saw me being born. He looked at me, a squalling thing caught slippery and wiggling in Tookie's hands.

Back in town, Daddy was beneath the backside of Judy Carter's Oldsmobile, wrenching the stubborn clamp from a rusted muffler. He told himself stories of his boyhood while he worked. He lifted the new muffler in place, new bolts gleaming on the ground like jewels.

He remembered a neighborhood kickball game on Ohio Street; Luciella Tanner (he kissed her once); riding his bike to the corner store for a pickle every Friday, twenty-five cents; sitting between Aunt Jo and Uncle Peck in morning church service, Uncle Peck's cologne bearing down on him like roses at a funeral; the fight that nearly cost him his life.

He held the muffler in place with one hand and tightened the bolt with the other. The screwdriver slipped and made a new wound at the fleshy base of his hand. His skin was shocked white where the screwdriver had been. Then blood trickled out in a dotted line. Daddy dabbed at it with a clean corner of one of his rags, wiped the sweat from his brow, where that zigzag scar was, and kept to his work.

Mama Minnie tore the pockets and ties off her apron and placed them between Mama's legs. She used the largest piece of the cloth to wrap around me, then placed me in Lucy Goode Brown's arms.

But Mama couldn't stop bad thoughts from clotting in her brain. There was already a sorrow cloaked around her head that she couldn't shake.

Mama Minnie cut the cord with her pocketknife.

Mama cried.

Mama Minnie pointed toward the field where she had been born, like she knew the exact spot, like she remembered.

"That's when a body worked," she said. Then she said *"Hush!"*

And we all grew quiet, like there was something more to listen to. Mama Minnie's words were like prayer. Granny Tookie stroked Mama's head. She caressed her arms, massaged her neck and shoulders, and finally entwined their fingers.

When it was time, Granny broke the silence.

"She's a pretty little pullet of a thing."

She stroked the wet strands of my hair. My birth watered down the boy-spell that Kee Kee had cast on her, but that didn't suppress the twinge of regret in her heart.

"Girl, girl, girl," she said.

She looked toward the ridge for help—the wind, the sky, the Lord.

They packed Mama into the backseat of the Plymouth, leaving behind the afterbirth until Mama Minnie struggled back out of the car, retrieved a grubbing hoe, and covered the birthing spot with a few turns of the blade.

Kee Kee was still, though his insides were flipping like grub worms, like fish.

Granny was also silent again, readying herself for the descent of the old haunts. She could feel them coming before she even pressed on the gas.

Mama rested her head on the seat and kept me warm, though I could feel a coldness brewing even then.

A light summer wind picked up, whipped through the hickory at the end of the lane. The heavens grew dark, as if a storm was churning, but the sky blued up quickly and we traveled in the red blaze of the day's last sunshine.

Kee Kee tried to remain quiet. Mama didn't look like our mother at all. She whispered incoherently through chapped lips, feeble as he had ever seen her. He wanted her to play jacks with him or read him a book, but she never did those things again.

He thought I looked like he could twang me with his thumb and forefinger and I would collapse to dust, a tiny little thing, gold as egg yolk. He looked out the back window, watching the homeplace shrink from big to the size of a postcard to a tiny speck. He tried to count trees, but there were too many to count, too many to name. Maple, oak, birch, syca-more, hickory. He watched dust roll out behind us and saw the road change from gravel to pavement. He wanted to say, "Hey, Mama, look at that," every time Granny drove the Plymouth past something of interest to him, but he knew he couldn't. The car felt like church. But before long he could not resist.

"Mama, look at them cows."

He pointed to a calf. The mother cow extended a black-ish-pink tongue, chewed her cud, and looked toward the car.

"I see them."

Mama's voice was raspy and dry. Kee Kee watched the cloth fall away from me a little as Mama's head lolled off to the side and her eyes closed.

"Your sister done wore her out," Mama Minnie said over the seat.

Sister. Kee Kee had to ready his mouth for that word. He had never had one before, a sister, so he watched out the window and placed his tongue against his teeth, whispering a hissing *sss* before he said it out loud to himself.

"S-s-sister."

At that moment, each of us—there were six of us then—was enveloped in our own separate haunt. Yet we were one, sharing past and future. Even my father, back in town work-ing, he was with us, too. Later, he would say that at the moment I was born he looked up and watched a flock of blackbirds turn away from the wind like sails on a kite.

Granny floored the Plymouth through the countryside. Trees and houses whirred by the open windows. Late in the after-noon, when the car crossed Mission Creek Bridge back into town, the sky was barely pinking up against the knobs.

Somewhere in the pending night, Old Man Lucien's dog

caught the possum's scent again. Her eyes flashed. She gave a determined snort and set off through the woods.

Granny remained quiet. The last shimmer of daylight fell warm and yellow on the dashboard and danced across her face before it vanished. The water in the creek curled and rolled toward the car as if to greet us, like a hundred tongues whispering *home, home, home.*

Sky. Blood. Bone. Breath.

Lucy

Thunder rattles the windows, and Lucy wakes from a restless sleep, thinking of her husband. Five days ago she gave birth in the squash patch, but for now she prefers the satisfaction of old memories knocking against one another. Let the baby wait. Everyone behind that bedroom door can just wait.

Joe Brown came to Opulence looking for work when he was twenty-one years old. He went with a few girls before settling on her. She and Joe, they'd had their first date, if you could call it that, at a church social. They held their chicken dinners awkwardly on paper plates and sat side by side in wooden fold-up chairs. They tried to talk, but neither of them was very good at it. She was surprised that he wanted to meet up with her again.

"Listen, maybe we can eat, talk some more or something," he stuttered out. "I sure want the chance . . ."

"Yes," she said, quicker than she'd meant to.

Yes. It came out like a scream. And she knew the moment he smiled at her, even before he opened the door and invited her into his pickup truck, that there would be no turning back. She wore the same pink dress she'd had on that day in the churchyard. They went into town for ice cream at the drug store, and then rode in his pickup to the countryside to watch the moon and stars and to talk.

"Pleasant night," she said, looking up at the sky out the truck window. Trying too hard. Wondering how a city woman might say it.

A silver cross hung from his rearview mirror. The entire truck smelled of grease and sweat. Bird shit and mud sullied the windows. Back then, most everything he owned was in that truck. He took on odd jobs, but it was clear even then that Joe knew his way around an engine best.

"You smell nice," he said. He looked her in the eye, then looked away and cleared his throat.

Lucy laughed. "You tongue-tied as I am."

"I suppose so." He blushed.

They stepped from the truck into the chilly night. The air was electrified with night sounds—birds, frogs, crickets. Lucy winced and grabbed at her elbows. He put his arms around her, and they stood out in the cool air quietly, without struggling to speak.

"Maybe we're thinking too hard," Lucy said.

"Might be."

Joe's headlights beamed out into the woods. Rain began to beat at their scalps and shoulders. He pulled her in close to him.

He leaned in to kiss her, but she said, "Hoot owls out there. You hear them?"

He nodded. "You don't hear nothing like this where I'm from."

They stood quiet and hugged up in the sheeting rain until Joe said, "Let me get you home."

Wet and in love in one instant, married the next.

Sometimes now, after more than twenty years married,

Joe Brown sulls up like a bullfrog for a few days and doesn't say much. Homesick again, Lucy figures. He's trying to rearrange in his own mind just where home is.

Home where you born and raised?

Home where your mama's at?

Home where your wife is. Simple as eyes in your head. *You ain't belonged to that city for a long time, Joe. You belong to me.*

When she thinks of that rainy day now, Lucy remembers her cheek on his shoulder and the way something deep down inside her cracked open and was set free.

Rain beats against the windowpane of her bedroom. Suddenly Lucy smells squash. The blossoms, the yellow bodies curved, long-necked, and graceful, their fullness heavy on the vines by her head as she pushed her baby girl out.

She reaches down beneath the covers and is somewhat surprised that her belly, the taut mountain that had cradled her child, is wobbly and loose and back to being hers alone. Aware of her hip bones now, the tightness of her engorged breasts, she scoots to Joe's side of the bed, rolls away from his cold spot, misses that extra weight in front that has kept her oddly off balance for all these months. Now she feels hollow, a drained riverbed. She liked being pregnant. When Kee Kee was born she settled into this loss for weeks, refusing to come out of her bedroom, not eating. But eventually that dreariness slipped away.

She stands, only half-steadily. Her body is stiff, a little weak. She smells her own blood, hears her family moving about the house, the rain's tap-tapping. The window is already cracked a few inches. Lucy opens it fully and leans into the sill. Outside, a muddy pool of water forms at the end of the walkway like a tiny river. Lucy Goode Brown, who will later consider herself too busy for daydreaming, is taken by the birds calling to one another in the distance. The clamor of her own house grows as faint as secrets while she lets her mind ride the night.

Neighbors are out on their porches, fanning themselves with newspapers and cardboard scraps. Gnats and mosquitoes have come along with the rain; the sound of skin being slapped echoes from house to house. This rain will bolster their gardens, and they will all celebrate the fat tomatoes and the second round of kale greens now holding water in curly leaves. Pink zinnias and red begonias will perk up bright. On up the road, across Mission Bridge, old black farmers in the farther reaches of the country are nodding with the quiet pleasure a good rain brings. They have crossed their arms, chests swollen with pride, their snowy heads held up high beneath the shelter of barns and porches. Some will stand fully in the rain and let it take them, as she and Joe did when they were courting. Crops will green up again. The family garden is glistening wet, the remaining squash turning graceful yellow necks toward the downpour.

A girl and a boy chase each other around in circles up and down the road. The trees are full of rain; when the girl reaches for a branch they both get wet. The girl's hair has gone home already in the dampness, bushing out around her plaits. Can't quite make out whose child she is, one of the Jenkins girls, maybe. Lucy thinks, only briefly, of her newborn girl in the arms of her mother on the other side of that door. This baby is the last one.

A woman with a coat over her head trudges downhill. Lucy can't see her face. *Could be me.* She imagines herself with her mother's raincoat over her head, unnoticed, walking uphill in the downpour, across Mission Bridge, away from here. *An invisible Goode woman, imagine that.* Her eyes tear up, spill out their own warm water from thimble-sized oceans.

She registers the ruckus of evening again—the end of supper, voices, chairs being scooted out. Behind that door are clothes to wash, a white sudsy sink of dishes, children to feed, a husband to love, a mother to please, a grandmother to praise . . .

Raindrops on her skin? Sweat? Nice and quiet and cool. She sees herself splashing around like a muddy child—free, free. Then she returns to her bed.

Joe's dresser drawer is cockeyed, a few of his socks bunch up at the edge of the wood and hang over. A pile of work clothes clutter the floor. His pajamas are thrown over the back of a chair in the corner. Lucy breathes in the moist air that settles around her, looks around at the mess, shakes her head.

She will scold him later, when he is beside her in bed. "Joe Brown," she'll say. "Daddy," she'll say, then stop and smile. "Baby," she'll begin again, "with Kee Kee and this new one and Mama and Ma Minnie getting up in age . . . and, Daddy . . . Sugar, could you just do a little bit for yourself?" She'll place her fingers together like she's just asking for something tiny, just a pinch of something. She'll cut her eyes just right. "Joe . . . Will you? . . . I'll do the rest . . . Ain't I always done the rest?" She won't know what to say really, exactly how to say it. Then Joe will get that sad look on his face like he's preparing for a quarrel, and she'll smooth it all out with a light kiss on his collarbone. That place right there, like a little hill and valley where she likes to rest her lips. Her lips won't be dry then. They'll be the tiniest bit wet. And then he'll know what she means. They can't make love yet but that one kiss right there will tide him over, smooth everything out like an iron to a sheet. From behind her she'll scoop his rough hands around her jiggle of a waist and he'll press his heart to her back. That's how they'll sleep.

Remember when we got married? Came up to this room

and didn't come out for a week. Had your big old eyes right here for me to look into. That scar running clean through your eyebrow like my very own beacon. We were legs, four arms, one silly heart. That's what we were.

She laughs. Oh, how that sounds.

Now you scattered out all over, your head turned in every direction. Fixing something for that one, mowing for this one, working on somebody's car. Your heart? Don't know where your heart is. Suppose it's still mine, but seems like you belong to all of creation. And don't get me wrong, I would wash your dirty drawers 'til kingdom come if you could save me from this. This . . . drowning. Feel like I'm in Mission Creek. Just about gone. Circle me back to that old feeling again, Baby. Just once, Daddy. And don't think I wouldn't do anything in the world for my babies, because I would. Mama and Mama Minnie too and . . .

Lucy considers climbing back out of bed to tidy the room, but she curls on her side and falls asleep.

Mama Minnie comes in at intervals and changes the padding between her legs, tests her forehead for fever. Bone tired, Lucy sleeps herself toward healing.

"Bout time to feed this baby," Minnie Mae says, and shakes Lucy's arm a little to rouse her. But Lucy sleeps on, her closed eyes darting back and forth. Mama Minnie wipes drool from her mouth and calls Tookie to change the pillowcases, which are sour with sweat.

The women work simultaneously. Mama Minnie wipes a streak of blood from Lucy's thigh. Tookie replaces the top sheet and quickly spreads a clean one back across Lucy. She smooths the fresh pillow and places it under her daughter's head. Would crawl right into Lucy's sickbed and hold her across her heart if she could.

"Reckon Joe can stay here with her?" Tookie pats the pillow where her son-in-law will sleep.

"Long as he ain't got no man notions."

Tookie says nothing. Thinks, *clean daughter, fresh room.*

Lucy stirs, but doesn't dare open her eyes.

First time Tookie met Joe Brown, she thought something was funny about him, with that scar above his eye—and the timbre of his voice told her he wasn't from around here. Scar always looked like it was from a brawl of some kind, clean and straight as a razor. She didn't want that kind of man for her daughter. Don't no woman need a fighting man: once he's done whipping up on somebody else, he'll turn on his woman. But she didn't see that kind of meanness in Joe's spirit now. He turned out to be a true, good thing. It was clear he was a tender man when he bathed Kee Kee or took Lucy's hand and kissed it in the palm. All a woman needs in this world is a tender man.

"In my time, a man was out of a woman's bed least six weeks," Minnie Mae says.

Tookie hums yes. Thinks: *Husband belongs in bed with his wife, even in times like this.* "You think she looks alright?" She squeezes both of Lucy's feet. She touches her daughter every chance she gets. A body needs touch, she thinks. Woman needs love hands on her. "She's alright, ain't she?" she asks again.

Minnie Mae doesn't answer, she's already said her piece.

Minutes later, in a dream, Lucy climbs a ridge on the path to a pond. Her plaits are freed out around her head like rat snakes set loose. Her palms are splayed open, held skyward as if in prayer. A gust of wind ripples across the water, and the mysteries it holds are more important than any single thing Lucy can think of. She quells the urge to jump in, to try to swim to the other side just to see if she can. She stays by the pond until dusk, then through nightfall. She sits on the water's edge as it churns and rises, threatening flood. Ants crawl up her calves, and there is a snail on her knee, a frog nestled in the crook of her arm. She tries to shoo them off, but more come. It is after she grows resistant to the pinching bite of the mosquitoes, after it no longer seems unusual to have the frog there, after she becomes accustomed to the slimy trail the snail leaves as it climbs her thigh, and after the dance of lightning bugs begins in her hair that stillness settles in her. The water continues to chop, but in the darkness her own churning stops and her attention folds inside out. The night is so black she can't see, and though she can feel every living thing on her body, she is really somewhere else, somewhere close to the moon. She has almost lost herself. A barred owl hoots. Above her, an endless heaven of stars, a world larger and more glorious than herself. Above her, the very sky shifts from blue black to deep purple, changing with the night.

Lucy wakes, not knowing how long she has slept this time. Sheets are stale again. She doesn't remember her dream exactly, but her heart races. She shifts her weight to the side. The day is nearly gone, a fleshy orange out the window, even though it's still raining. Lucy hears the baby crying, the squall in her ear a sweet ache. Her breasts throb, then tingle, and she can already feel milk straining through her crusted nipples. She frees herself from her bra and milk comes first in slow drops, then faster, running down the rise of her belly and pouring into the crevice of her navel. She tries to stop it by bunching up the top sheet against her breasts, but her breasts shift just a little and high streams of milk squirt into the air. Later, when she thinks of herself like this, Lucy's skin will goose up at the miracle of motherhood.

Tookie raps at the door and then pushes it open with her

elbow. "Somebody's hungry," she says, and leans in to place the baby in Lucy's arms, but Lucy rolls over on her side.

"Come on now," Tookie says. "Every living thing got to eat." She bounces the baby against her own chest. The baby girl's sweet cheek nestled against her collarbone makes her dizzy with love.

Lucy rolls over and Tookie holds the baby out toward her, tries to place her in Lucy's arms again. Lucy pushes Tookie's hands away until the baby is back against her grandmother's chest.

"Come on, girl."

"She'll learn early then, won't she?" Lucy says.

"Learn what, Lucy? You ain't making sense." Tookie brings the baby closer. Everything living does have to eat, so the baby begins to kick, and the soft, almost pretty wail lofts up and out against the walls.

"Crazy," Tookie says to the baby. "Good thing we got bottles boiled and ready, cause your mama's crazy."

And there it is again: 1943 knock, knock, knocking on Tookie's head. The day Lucy was born. That beating she got. Who else would a child turn to but her mama? Who else but a mama would understand her child's hunger? Tookie rubs at her temples trying to get the headache to stop, trying to keep 1943 from knocking too hard. There are things to do. Her grandbaby needs her and so does her Lucy.

One tiny foot slips from the blanket and Tookie holds it in her hand for a few seconds, rubbing her thumb across each sweet toe. She opens the door and slips back into the hum of common sense in the rest of the house.

Lucy places her left hand on her breasts. Streams of clear blue milk drip down her side and over her right hand, which is below, between her legs.

When Mama Minnie steps back into the room to see the

sight of Lucy herself, it's clear to her that she has taken a sick spell of some sort, be it of mind or body. She wants to give it over to fever, but the baby still needs to be fed.

"Hold her feet," she says to Tookie, and pushes her full weight atop Lucy, holding her hands down, even with Lucy kicking and screaming.

"We got bottles," Tookie says, but takes her place at the bottom of the bed.

"Cow's milk for cows," says Mama Minnie.

Wrestling with her granddaughter makes Minnie Mae think of all the men she's fought in her life. Brought on fighting Macon Jones one year during hog-killing time when she was twelve, wrestling him for her own honey pot. She'd won, though—still a virgin when she married. Brought on knocking out that boy, Possum Briggs, that time when he'd called her out of her name and slapped her when they were swimming in the creek, and how scared her mama was that she'd hang for giving that old white boy a black eye. Brought on plenty.

Minnie Mae puts a cold rag to Lucy's forehead, then presses down on her arms hard enough to leave a bruise. Lucy thrashes, cries out "No!" again and again, tries to cover her head with the sheet. Tookie holds her feet, her own stomach in knots, a sick feeling coming quickly, no matter how hard she tries to calm her nerves. Minnie Mae calls for Joe to come situate the baby so his child can eat.

Joe Brown holds the baby awkward as any man would, though he is a bit more sure with this one, his second. His hands look more natural holding a wrench or pliers, and lately even an ax or a saw, even pictured himself holding the reins of a mule behind a plow or a disc. Sometimes he is surprised by the contrast of his tough, dry skin against Lucy's back when he massages her shoulders, and now, cupping his soft baby girl against her mother's breast, he feels as though he needs to ask permission.

When the baby latches to her mother her face goes peaceful and satisfied. Lucy struggles, breathing heavy like she's in a fight, like she's running from a long ways off, but once the baby has nursed, she quiets down and goes back to sleep.

Later in the night, when Joe crawls into the cold space beside her, he notices right away where Lucy's hands are, and says, "Baby, you okay? Need anything?"

"Need a lot."

"You want some ice water? There's tea . . ."

"No."

"Hungry?"

"Not for what you talking about."

Joe Brown clears his throat; even in the dark he can see Lucy's hand moving around. Smell of women's blood is filling up the room. He lies in the dark, listening to her quick breathing beside him.

At her funeral years later, when they have closed the coffin and are carrying Lucy out of Mission Creek Baptist Church, when the glint of copper on the coffin catches sunlight, even in his grief, Joe will suddenly remember this night and how Lucy's smell took up the entire room. And he will remember rain ping-pinging on the window, how much he loved her and how he could never have left her side, no matter how crazy she was—least folks thought she was crazy; he won't be sure even then; could have been some kind of sign from God for all he knows—and he will remember this night and how they were quiet like that for a long time, how even with the clouds he could see the outline of trees through the window. He will remember this time and how her hands remained on herself in those places, her fingers caked with blood and milk.

When company arrives a few days later, Minnie Mae, in her church pearls and a touch of wine-red lipstick, posts herself in a wingback chair beside the front door. She kisses some of the women on the cheek, grasps the hands of others. She eyeballs some, but greets them politely and directs each woman toward Lucy, who is sitting almost motionless in a rocking chair across the room.

"Get yourself some lemonade and go on out back," she says to the children.

"In the kitchen," she says to the men, and nods her head in the kitchen's direction.

Outside, this night hangs like a cloak, hot and moist enough to wring out like a wet tea towel. The rain has stopped for now, and the heat causes steam to rise from the ground like smoke. A sliver of moon glows through the clouds.

Lucy is at the far end of the living room, almost sullen in the rocking chair, holding the baby in a receiving blanket. Tookie stands behind Lucy with her arms keeping the chair from rocking, keeping Lucy and the new baby safe and immobile. She says nothing, but nods once or twice as the women come one by one.

"Pretty little thing."

"Law me, look at that."

"What a bolt from the blue," they say.

"What'd you name her?"

Tookie holds the back of the chair, more peaceful behind her shield. If she looks them in the eye for too long, 1943 comes humming back. She's a long-necked girl again with her belly six-months swollen. Cast out of the church choir, told she can't talk to her friends. Shame washes over her still.

Back over Tookie's left shoulder, through the haze of insects drawn to the porch light, Kee Kee is playing in the yard. He has been joined by one of the Jenkins boys and they are running around the poles of the clothesline.

German chocolate cake, lemon meringue pie, pimento cheese sandwiches, sugar cookies, mints, and peanuts. Joe has moved the furniture back to make way for the crowd. Children turn noisy at the sight of dessert, and are quickly shooed out into the backyard by their mothers. Girls go wide-eyed at the baby. Boys sneak extra cookies or a paper cup of lemonade and clack the back screen door behind them.

Lucy rocks the baby, answers the same question a blue million times, hears men's voices ebb and flow in the kitchen. The house is alive with sound. She grins when she hears Joe's words rise and fall in the talking: *Go fishing before long. No, not all night. I know you right. Man, I'm telling you. Kak's Chevrolet.*

"Girl, how'd you do it? How you survive that field?" women her age ask. Some of them she hasn't seen since high school.

"Woman always does what she has to." Lucy finds a chortle somewhere inside her to make light, but even while she's throwing her head back, it sounds to her like some other woman's laugh rising up out of her chest. She places a hand on her throat just to be sure.

"Where's that man of yours done run off to?" one of them finally asks.

"He ain't run no further than the kitchen," Lucy says, and cocks her head to listen to the men. Ah, there it is. Joe's voice soothing her, even far off like that, rising up and going down low out there in the kitchen. Lucy thinks of Joe's deep laugh, his tender whisper in her ear, the deep growl of his snoring.

Her hand a little shaky, Tookie steps forward and takes the baby clothes, bottles, and pink-wrapped gifts from visitors and places them on the coffee table. She refills the lemonade and piles more sugar cookies on a serving platter before she returns to safety behind the rocking chair. Some of the women stare: Lucy in the rocker, holding that baby and looking off into the air at nothing in particular, and Tookie, with her hands gripped tightly to the back of the chair and her head dropping every time anybody tries to catch her glance. It's an odd sight.

Both doors have been opened enough times that the flies are starting to settle in the house. Two of them are taking turns landing on the baby's cheeks and eyes. Others are swarming around the pie. A yellow jacket buzzes through the living room, and gnats fly around the lemonade. One hums in Lucy's ear. She turns her head but doesn't even swat at it. A fly lands on the baby again, feasting on the corner of her eye. The baby blinks. Lucy just watches the fly rubbing its front legs together, a tiny hungry tongue. Tookie reaches in and shoos it from the baby's head.

The fan in the corner of the living room blows hot air around. A few more men have joined the others huddled in the sweaty kitchen, where they find Joe Brown on the floor under the table, repairing a wobbly leg.

"Congratulations, put her there," one man says, pulling Joe to his feet and shaking his hand.

"She done dragged me over here. You know how the women are," another says. "How you doing, Joe. Man, you getting any sleep?"

Joe Brown shakes his head, swipes his brow and his neck. *You know how the women are.* The men are still talking and laughing, but Joe isn't listening fully. He wants to answer back "No! I sure as hell don't know how the women are!" But he knows the man wasn't expecting a real answer. Men pat him on his sticky back. His silver-tongued beginnings are almost forgotten; they nod at each other with this thought in their minds. It's only when he talks fast or calls up some citified story that they remember where he's from.

After everyone has had a bite to eat, Mama Minnie taps her cane against the floor three times. The room quiets and she walks into the center like a preacher woman and says, "God sure does make a way, don't he?"

Sister Betty shouts, "Amen!" and everyone claps.

"We sure do feel blessed to have her," Mama Minnie points to the baby, "and blessed to have so many of the Lord's servants with us here today." She bows and then says, "Thank you Jesus," and looks up at the crowd.

One of the younger women whispers to the others and they cover their mouths. People applaud again, and a few boys who have come back for more food whistle through their fingers. One of the men pulls his tall, lanky boy into the kitchen by the arm and threatens to whip him in front of everybody. A few of the women look to see if Lucy will address the group, but when she lowers her head toward the baby, the room turns noisy again.

People continue milling around the house, talking among themselves, drinking every last drop of lemonade, eating every cookie, every last damn peanut. When the baby begins to cry, her tiny mouth bowing out into a perfect thimble, a few women turn and smile, tilt their heads to the side. One of them says with delight, "Ain't that the cutest thing you ever did see?" But when the baby reaches a full, soft cry, Lucy begins a howl.

Tookie rubs her shoulders, but she is inconsolable.

Joe comes from the kitchen, kneels down beside the chair. "Baby, you alright?"

Lucy's lips are quivering, her chest heaving. She lets out a moan, cries harder, and gasps for breath. She does not stop.

The crowd is now quiet again. Some of the women admire Joe's hand on Lucy's leg, and feel the imaginary weight of a man's hand on their own knees. Others are whispering among themselves.

"Crazy heifer!"

"Well if that don't beat all."

Lucy rocks back and forth in the chair, Tookie reaches in to take the baby, Joe strokes Lucy's knee like a man who doesn't know what else to do, but before he can intervene, before Tookie can pull the baby safely into her own arms, before Mama Minnie can cross the room, the baby rolls from Lucy's lap, rolls like a can of lard, like a wad of fabric or a cumbersome quilt, like a rolling pin or a small sack of new potatoes, and makes a light thud on the plank floor like something being cast away.

There is one wide-eyed look on every face in the room. A great communal hush rises up, and for a few seconds no one says a word. Then all attention turns to Tookie, who falls to her knees, scoops the baby into her arms, and then almost topples headfirst when she tries to get back to her feet. A few women grab the hands of their children, lower their heads, and leave quietly.

When the front door flies open and people start to step off the porch, Mama Minnie sees a large woman from church, Francine Clark, standing at the edge of the yard holding a Pyrex dish. Francine steals a nervous glance toward Mama Minnie, then nods to her and turns back toward the road without coming in, without leaving what she brought. Mama Minnie, who still has one ear on the commotion but her eye on Francine Clark, follows her wide hips down the worn path in the grass, and even in the midst of the chaos says aloud to herself, "Something always been funny bout that woman."

Afraid she might be hurt, Tookie pulls back the blanket and runs her fingers across the baby's head in search of lumps, looks for bruises. The baby stops crying. Kee Kee watches his mother and watches the remaining neighbors watching his mother. "Mama," he hollers out, but Lucy acts as if she doesn't hear him. She ignores her firstborn. She buries her eyes in her hands and bites her lip, but tears are streaming down her face and dripping off her chin. Joe rubs her arm.

"Let me get you back to bed," he says. And the women are hushed again by the love in his voice. Lucy raises her head, and for a moment her face is so twisted and puffy that Joe barely recognizes her. She stands, wilts, leans into Joe, and he leads her through the maze of onlookers to their bedroom, where he places her in the bed and pulls a sheet up over her.

Nobody speaks a word until Mama Minnie says, "Here, y'all get some of this caramel cake before you leave." And Tookie, with the baby still pressed against her, rushes over to help wrap pieces of cake in tinfoil with her free hand.

As everyone leaves, a clap of thunder sounds in the distance and they scatter toward their homes. Rain pours out in buckets. Elders return to their front porches, children search for june bugs. Whip-poor-wills serenade a young couple who dare to make love up against the roughness of a toolshed, way out in the dark. Somewhere a dog barks for a child to come back out to play. But the baby, this Yolanda—born out in the field in the old way—and her mother, Lucy Goode Brown—a plumb crazy woman—are never far from every lip. And poor Joe Brown. She's lucky as sin to have him. Wonder if he don't pack up and leave. On this night, and for a long time to come, every tongue stirs.

Inside the Goode house, Mama Minnie opens up her Bible, thinking of a few soothing words to say. Then, just as quick, she decides to keep them to herself until morning.

She reads Psalm 46:

> God is our refuge and strength, an ever-present help
> in trouble. Therefore we will not fear, though the
> earth give way and the mountains fall into the heart

of the sea, though its waters roar and foam and the mountains quake with their surging.

She prays before settling into bed. Girl just needs her time. Her mind drifts back to that Clark woman out in the yard, big old body balanced on them little feet, holding her dish and not saying a word. Like she didn't have a lick of sense.

Tookie stares at the ceiling in her own bedroom, presses the nubby surface of her bedspread, then smooths it out with her fingers. She repeats this until she has pressed some of the worry out of her head, a tiny moment of respite before worry comes back. Something bad has done come over her child.

Kee Kee gets into his red pajamas by himself. He kisses his mother, his father, and his brand-new sister before going to his room, wishing he could sleep with them.

"Sleep tight, little man," his father says. "Good night, Kevin."

His mother says nothing.

Lucy and Joe spoon against one another, the baby curled against her mother's breast.

By the time the house rests, Mama Minnie has already left her burden of the day and tied up her hair, and is under her sheet snoring.

Everyone is asleep when Lucy cries again. Her tears come as easy as breath. She touches the child's face as it nurses, and then pinches the baby's nostrils together. She does this as she feels Joe nestled against her back.

How simple life is. Silly how it works, really.

She could starve the child of air and even Joe, who is snoring gently in her ear, would never know. She watches her daughter struggle for breath, watches her bright eyes widen until the legs kick and she lets go of the nipple. Lucy does it again until she can feel the baby trying to fling her head free, then she releases and listens to her child settle into being able to breathe again. A hurried in and out. In. Out. She listens for a long time, only the teeniest bit of panic rising in her until the baby's breath is in rhythm with her own again.

In truth, Lucy can hear the breathing of the entire house. The out. The in. Out. In. They are loud: one big choir singing out survival in the night. Her eyes race around the room. She can smell the wildness of her own milk.

Little Bird.

Francine

By late December, the pin oak and birch are drooped like weeping willows. Snow is on the ground, and Joe Brown is in Francine Clark's yard, clearing a path to her car. She watches him through the window, sees him bending to pick up brush. Each branch glistens thick with the weight of ice. Talk of weather has replaced the resounding thud of Joe and Lucy's baby being dropped to the floor.

Francine had been curious about the Goode baby, born out there in that squash field, so when she heard about the gathering from the mailman, she made her best oyster casserole and carried it up to that house. But when she heard those people inside mingling around, eating and laughing, her legs went stuck. She didn't know what had happened when they all left at once, but she heard the women talking. Those women, always with their tongues flying about somebody.

Then she saw Minnie Mae Goode at the door, and caught just a glimpse of Lucy inside, with her dark, unruly hair spewed in all directions, and Joe Brown leading her off. In some strange way, Lucy was still beautiful, but she looked older, more gaunt, haggard. Exhausted by the sight, Francine turned to leave, then ducked back behind Joe Brown's tool-shed until everyone had scattered. She couldn't see inside the

Goode house, but she imagined them in there milling about
from room to room. The six of them. All filled with some great
love for each other. Normal, except for Lucy, tired and startled
as a cat, looking wildly out of place. Francine stood in the rain
for a long time that afternoon. Things moved in her gut. Feelings she'd never known. *Jealousy*, that's what she'd call it now.
The strength of the Goode family. She was stunned at the idea
of losing Sonny before the two of them had a chance at a real
family. She would never have a family, not one like that, with
a man at its center.

A baby in the field and all that chaos afterward. Francine
wonders what Joe thinks about all of it now. His arms, hands
are working like a machine, scooping up broken limbs and
placing them into the burlap bag he drags behind him through
the snow, clearing the sidewalk. His eyes and head are darting
all around—to the tops of the trees where birds are gathering
in black clusters, to the hills still whitecapped.

There's a rabbit at the edge of the yard, and every so often
it wriggles its nose and hops in Joe's direction. Joe looks as
though he's not paying attention, but he's the kind of man who
sees everything. When he gets done clearing sticks and snow
from the path, he'll drop a slip of paper in Francine's mailbox
with his requested pay written in his careful script, and she'll
mail him a check first thing tomorrow. Before he leaves, he
stands with his hands on his hips and watches the rabbit, still
sniffing and hopping, looking for water maybe or food, and
then Joe climbs into his truck and is gone like he came, without bothering to knock on Francine's door. This pleases her.
She wishes everyone acted like this.

Long after Joe Brown's truck can no longer be seen or
heard, Francine presses her ear to the wall and listens to the
muted scratch of squirrels. She has spent the ten years since

Sonny died training herself to enjoy the occasional rustlings of some creature, or a twig scratching the window, a little bit of low music, even the company of the tomcat she feeds on the back porch, but no people. People come plagued with disappointment.

When gray-eyed Sonny Clark, considered a prize among the women, returned to Opulence married to Francine—citified, dark, and big boned—all eyes were already on the house before they'd even moved in. And the gaze has held steadfast, even since Sonny's passing.

In town they say she's an odd one—hincty and soft—all that weight, those small, useless hands and feet. Even the skinniest women in town, though thin as runner beans, would make two of big old Francine Clark on any given workday.

Francine runs her hand down the wall and crosses the living room to the kitchen. The swish of her fleshy thighs and the occasional skittering inside the plaster are all the sound in her world on this night.

In the kitchen, she stirs black walnuts into cocoa, confectionary sugar, and butter. Gospel twangs through her radio, and though she doesn't particularly enjoy the country music, the words soothe her:

> Pass me not, oh gentle Savior
> Hear my humble cry
> While on others Thou art calling
> Do not pass me by
>
> Savior, Savior
> Hear my humble cry
> While on others Thou art calling
> Do not pass me by

Chocolate bubbles up and splatters against the sides of the pan. She stirs and takes in a breath deep enough to lift her large breasts. She hums along to the music, her voice lifting out *Savior . . . Savior*. She puts the teapot on.

It was just Sonny's time—her rational mind knows it, her God-fearing heart knows it—but that part of her that remains empty, the part Sonny used to fill up, still nudges her into believing that dying was something he could have prevented if he had loved her enough.

Rained hard like that July night at the Goodes' house when the whole town lined up to see the famous Goode baby who was born in the field. Hear ye, hear ye, she thinks now. Come see Yolanda, the wonder baby born amidst the squash.

That other storm though. Power lines down. Her man up before daylight. Even when day came, the sky was still dark and the clouds full. She shoved a paper sack filled with a piece of chocolate cake, a fried chicken breast, and two slices of light bread into his hands.

Or did I just give him one slice that morning?

"And where's my sugar?" he asked before he went.

The memory of that kiss makes her cheek warm.

She pours the remains of the walnut kernels into the batter.

Saw lightning strike. A beautiful thing, lightning, zigging and zagging like . . .

Pictures of heaven in her King James Bible, her Sonny, surrounded by light like a halo.

"Struck by lightning, what were the chances of that?" one of the men who dragged Sonny into the living room said.

"And living?" another added.

. . . lit up like fireworks on the Fourth.

. . . like Jesus.

Francine adds more confectionary sugar to the candy.

They came in, two of them, wet and dirty, and placed Sonny on the sofa. He was groaning, his face twisted to one side like he'd had a stroke.

Smell of burnt flesh, like meat cooking. Toes of his shoes blown out by the force of the current, his clothes shambled down to his underclothes. Those men taking little glances around like they were being let in on a secret.

"I still feel it go clean through me," Sonny told her. He held his hands out to her. "My fingers and toes, my arms . . ." He hollered out in the night in pain. Doctor came, said he'd be alright. Sonny coiled up like a baby, laid up on her breast.

"I can't go back out there," he said, just like a scared boy. And she held him like that, comforted him like that, like some child. "I can't go," he said.

But he had. He went back to working on the power lines, came back to himself. And then just when Francine had gotten some Sonny back, some Sonny, enough to satisfy her, all was lost again. He just lay down and died, took something as simple as a headache one night and died. Aneurysm, they'd said.

Fought off a lightning bolt for no reason.

She stirs the fudge again, feels a funny yank in her belly and mistakes it for grief.

Francine still looks all around this house like it doesn't quite belong to her. Small, somebody's fairy-tale house, bright yellow with brocade high-back chairs that barely hold her and an enormous sofa on swirling, claw-shaped feet. Everything is clean. When she's not reading the Bible she's scrubbing the sink, baseboards, floors.

Though Francine Clark's mind has just returned from a ten-year journey, she now stands in her own kitchen and is forty-six years and one hundred and twelve miles away. She is seven years old, in the house she grew up in on Oak Street in

Louisville. A large house, enviable by any standards, a house that could swallow the small house she lives in now at least twice, even three times, she suspects. It had a winding staircase that connected the two stories, and shiny hardwood floors.

Her honey-coated father, his navy suit fresh from the cleaners, and her mother, deep, deep, brown with a bit of Europe dancing in her face—the elongated nose, pointy chin, and thin lips. Francine, at the bottom of the stairs in her nightgown, looking up at her parents, swimming in the possibilities of her own future. But those memories they flit, glow with hope, and then disappear like lightning bugs.

Nervous breakdown: what a funny way to describe someone's malady. *Breakdown*, as though her mother were an appliance or a car.

Her smiling, popular mother, Helen Vernon. That mother who smelled like sun-ripened peaches, and kissed her father gently and softly, like his lips were something breakable; the mother who doted on her father as if she loved him more than any other thing. That mother, the one she had known until then, disappeared one day. Overnight, it seemed to Francine now.

Her hair lay on her shoulders, uncombed for days; later it would go for months, even years, because of her fear that combing it would be a signal for someone from the asylum to come and take her away. She refused to bathe because she was convinced she would drown. This woman, Francine's mother, who had once walked with confidence and grace, now cowered in a corner, balled into herself like a baby, afraid of something, afraid of everything.

Francine was fifteen years old when her father just left.

"Daddy can't take it no more," he said.

Francine stared at the ceiling while her father hugged her and cried. She felt the weight of him bearing down on her as he sobbed, but she held her arms straight down by her sides, like a soldier standing at attention. She refused to hug him back. She refused to cry.

After he left, and for years afterward, Francine simply existed in her mother's house. She refused to acknowledge or touch the woman, though sometimes she would sit at the top of the stairs or peek around the corner and watch her. It wasn't understanding that she sought—that was unfathomable. She just wanted to remember every sign of madness so that she could avoid it in her own life.

Helen Vernon fed herself sometimes, seeming normal, cooking a nice dinner for them both. Other times she discarded the whole meal in the trash, because she thought she saw roaches in it or believed it was poisoned. Francine's father brought food to the house every week, but Francine usually stayed out from underfoot when he arrived, observing him from across the room.

"Come give Daddy a hug?" he would ask her sometimes. But Francine refused his hugs, and ghosted herself somewhere in the house until she heard him turn the key and leave.

Francine hums it all back to where it came from and spoons chocolate onto wax paper. She has just licked her fingers clean when a sharp pain hits her stomach. She paces a few steps bent over and holds on to the counter, hoping this kink in her middle will work itself out. The kink subsides a little, and though she's startled and still feeling a little bit of pain, she straightens her dress and returns to the stove. She wipes splatters from the range with her dishcloth, then another stab strikes her. This one takes her to her knees.

As she lies down to rest on the linoleum, Francine notices a spot of dirt that she's somehow missed, a tiny spot, size of a half-dollar, shadowed by the table leg. She tries to get at it with her finger.

The teapot whistles.

She cooks for church members when there's occasion—a funeral, a baptism, a baby born—but she doesn't talk much. She is merely Sonny's wife: *That woman*. Still a stranger after all these years. She cherishes this. Folks don't bother strangers much; they just let them be. She doesn't want anyone clamoring around—but she does think about calling on somebody now . . . until she remembers people pouring out of Minnie Mae Goode's house into the July heat like bugs, carrying the story with them. She wants no part of that, even if her gallbladder is bursting.

When the pain lessens again, Francine pulls herself up on all fours. *Francine Lynette Clark, get yourself in order.* She stands, though she keeps her back humped over, and places a tea bag inside her China cup. She pours a bit of hot water, dowses the bag several times. She leaves the fudge cooling on the counter and the remnants in the pan scorching. The cabinet door is still open. That spot on the floor. These things taunt her. She manages to ease herself into a high-backed chair. She tries to relax her muscles, rubs at the small of her back, her side. The tea scalds her throat as it goes down. Her wedding band still gleams on her finger. Sometimes just looking at it calms her nerves.

Must be ten people standing on top of me.

Something I ate?

Sonny Clark, your wife is vexed.

There are women who do this all the time, women who don't know where their babies came from, who have menstrual cycles all through their pregnancies, women who refuse to remember tragedy, women who were raped. Then there are women who live one life by day and another by night. It is not known which category Francine Clark is in, so each resident in town puts her where they want her. Some will shift her to the double-life category, others will place her neatly in the box labeled *Rape*, but nobody knows for sure.

Some of the women will later say they noticed that she had gained more weight, but nobody had expected she was pregnant. Pregnant was the last thing they thought she could ever be. All except Minnie Mae Goode, who had rightly said, no more than six months ago, during her own family's chaos: "Something funny bout that woman, there." But even she had dismissed it as a sign of melancholy.

Some will say she knew. Some will say she couldn't have known. That if she had, she would have called in some of Sonny's people, even though she doesn't speak to them. No woman in her right mind would willingly do this—a scared teenager maybe, but not some old widow woman. Not in these modern times. Word will make its way: Francine Clark, church-going widow woman, calls the life squad for a bellyache and pops up with a black-headed baby girl. And brought the baby home swaddled in a blanket donated from some white church in town without a diaper pin nor a bassinet to her name.

"Old as she is? Ought to know better," the women will add.

And this is how Minnie Mae Goode's tribe will reclaim a little bit of their dignity. All that other talk from six months back, about Lucy Goode Brown having a baby amid the squashes, then losing her natural mind and whooping and hollering and dropping the baby right in the middle of the floor for all to see, will be put to rest for awhile. This new story fills up every dusty corner, every sly grin, every single drop of spit from every working tongue.

Mona's entrance into the world will make men's heads tilt in confusion, and cause old women to gossip with their hands on their hips. Over tea in one another's kitchens for the rest of winter they will speculate that a woman like Francine Clark is apt to run off or give the baby up.

"She don't know nothing," they'll say. "Ain't seen an honest day's work in her life."

When Francine brings her baby home, curtains and shades open and close all up and down the road until the strange car headed toward the Clark place is out of sight. Francine steps from the car and thanks the woman, her back straight but her eyes cast slightly downward. The plump, short white woman, a social worker from the hospital, watches as Francine walks gingerly across the icy sidewalk while balancing the baby, a handful of bottles, a box of baby powder, and five diapers, all provided by the hospital. A gust of cold wind picks up the edge of Francine's brown skirt tail and she grimaces. The hospital woman focuses in on the house. She has expected something different, something low-class and run down, especially with no father to be seen.

"Yoo-hoo, Miss Clark!" she yells from the window, her breath puffing out smoke from the cold. "You need help in?"

Snow is beginning to fall again.

"No, thank you kindly."

Francine trundles as quickly as her frame will let her, up the porch step and over the tomcat weaving around her ankles. She fumbles for her keys with one hand, and has the door open before the hospital woman is out of the car. A flock of sparrows takes off from the edge of the house and dusts the ground with fresh snow.

"Miss Clark!" The woman runs behind Francine like she's forgotten something. "Wait . . . I just wanted to wish . . ."

Francine Clark steps across her own threshold, steadies her senses against the stench of burnt chocolate that remains in her air, and quickly closes her door. She drops the supplies to the floor, then shrugs her arms out of her coat and lays it across one of the kitchen chairs. She uncovers Mona's face, traces the roundness of her cheeks and lips with her finger. A little bird, she is, a little bird. Francine can hear the white woman's boots crunch in the snow outside the door, the sound drifting away and away, up, out into the trees.

And then it hits her.

"Sonny, it's Christmas," she says. "And look what I've done."

1963

Summer Birds. Touch.
The Visitors.

Francine

By June, the summer birds have returned and this thing Francine Clark has done is still fresh on every tongue.

For months, even through winter, townswomen have come in small clusters to Francine's door, trying to exchange her secret for a peck or bushel of something. Francine keeps to her volition and greets them only by cracking the door the tiniest bit, or yelling, "Yes, who is it?" through three inches of fine oak.

"It's Sista So-and-So just thought you might need something, brought you some pie."

Sometimes it's Big Boy tomatoes, Silver Queen corn; diapers or milk.

"No thank you," Francine answers in return. They always knock a second time and Francine responds with silence.

Every Thursday, Francine places her baby on the floorboard of Sonny's Thunderbird and drives to Lexington. She pushes a grocery cart through a river of unfamiliar people, relieved that not a soul knows her name. She writes a check on Sonny's pension for canned goods, flour, sugar, rice, beans, sweet potatoes, and cornmeal. She delights in cans of sugar peas and square red-and-white boxes of instant mashed potatoes. Her list, written in her steady perfect cursive, reads:

June 6, 1963

Can of coffee
Bag of McIntosh apples
12 rib steaks (freeze half)
2 loaves of bread (on sale 29 cents)
Butter
Catsup
Cream of wheat (for Mona)
Fudge sandwich cookies
Fig Newtons
Eggs (one dozen)
Texas onions (one bag)
Cottage ham
5 pot pies
Grape preserves (two jars)
Milk (for Mona)

When she returns home, Francine promises herself for the umpteenth time that she'll get Joe Brown to cut the grass, to trim back the hedges. Joe Brown is a man who will not deny her peace. The grass whooshes against her leg. She balances a bag of groceries in the scoop of her left arm and Mona in her right. Her pocketbook is twisted around her wrist and she's leaning to one side. By the time she reaches the door, the paper sack falls to the ground. Francine is breathing heavy. Sweat trickles between her breasts. A large chunk of her perfect hairdo slips from the bun. She balances baby and pocketbook, places keys into the lock, turns the knob, and opens the door with her foot.

The piney smell of the freshly mopped floor greets them,

and Francine is immediately comforted. She lays Mona on the sofa and steps back out to gather her spilled bounty. She comes back inside and begins to put groceries away. She stuffs pot pies in the box freezer on the back porch, has to move around ice cream, frozen meat, and vegetables to make it all fit. Sonny, you did well with this one, she thinks, remembering the summer he enclosed the porch and bought the freezer. He'd been so pleased with his garden and thought she might want to can some of his green beans, his okra, his corn. He settled for freezing, put out porch chairs so they could keep watch over the garden and see the sun set over the ridge. She touches Sonny's favorite chair and feels the now worn edge of the wood. She looks out at the tall weeds where the garden spot used to be and then up toward the tree-covered hills. Nothing. There was a time when she would sit with him for hours, those little black bugs flying at the corners of her eyes, the evening chill creeping in—but she stayed, holding Sonny's hand while he gazed out at the land.

Francine slips back into the house and squeezes dried goods into the cupboard. Two boxes of macaroni tumble out to the floor. There are already two dozen eggs in the refrigerator and two gallons of souring milk, but she wedges the third in somehow.

Her square face is pensive, deliberate, focused. She feels the weight of this task fully, a tightening in her chest like a mighty bolt. She stands in the kitchen, catches her breath, and in the usual way when she becomes still, memory comes rushing in. Shame is buried beneath the folds of soft tissue around her stomach. She rubs her fat hands through the sweat on her neck and fidgets with her bra, where sweat drips down to her navel.

After her mother's breakdown, Francine burned all her dolls on the rubbish pile in the backyard. It seemed like the thing to do at the time, putting girlish things behind her. But then she saw a girl in her neighborhood playing with dolls on the porch in the afternoons. That's when she divided herself into two Francines—Francine Vernon, the lady of the house, looking after herself like a grown woman; and another Francine Vernon, hidden between her breasts, lurking somewhere beneath her ribs, curled up into the girl she was, longing for the rubbery touch of baby dolls in her hands.

Years later, when Sonny Clark (with his drawl and rust-colored complexion) came to the Kentucky Derby and bypassed all the pretty light-skinned girls to get to her, Francine knew her escape was finally within reach. She wasn't soft-eyed about Sonny then, just eager to leave home. When they first married, they rented a little apartment right off Broadway near 34th Street. It was nice to have a place that she could keep clean and cook in and enjoy without her mother's breakdown floating around her. Sonny was her passage out of darkness, but before long, her appreciation turned into love. So when he asked her to leave Louisville and move back to Opulence with him, she said yes, without hesitation she said yes.

In Francine's fifth year away, Helen Vernon died. The doctors said it was ovarian cancer. Helen hadn't seen a doctor in over twenty years. A short, gray-looking white man tried to tell Francine about the condition Helen Vernon was found in, but Francine didn't want to know. She patted his hand and said, "Thank you kindly," before he even finished the story.

She made the funeral arrangements. She placed a picture of her mother before the breakdown upon the closed silver casket. No one else attended. Not a relative, not a friend, not even her father, who called and told her that he had to work.

After being restored to its former dignity, the house sold quickly. It was all over, and Francine was relieved.

And now here she is, smothered beneath her own skin, smothered beneath all this worry. So she hoards food in the house, in her body, just like the mother squirrel inside the wall. The baby coos and, at this moment, seems content with herself, kicking her legs about. It's hard for Francine to believe that this little girl came from down there, from inside of her. Sonny is everywhere, washing his hands in the sink, opening the refrigerator. He comes to her, a milky apparition.

> What a friend we have in Je-sus,
> all our sins and griefs to bear!

She removes the pot of six boiled nipples and matching bottles from the stove.

> What a privilege to car-ry
> everything to God in prayer!

She screws tops on three of the bottles and places them in the cabinet.

> O what peace we often forfeit,
> O what needless pain we bear . . .

She pours milk into the other three, replaces the water, and turns on the stove.

> All because we do not car-ry,
> Ev-ery-thing to God in prayer.

She puts two fresh bottles in the refrigerator and one in the pan of water to warm. Cleans the counters. Hums.

Mona's legs are kicking harder now. The sounds she makes are sounds of agitation, but Francine remembers the five-pound sack of sweet potatoes in the trunk of the car. By the time she is out on the steps and into the driveway, Mona is in full squall, her cries so shrill that birds fly up from the trees in the front yard and circle before they land again. Francine retrieves the potatoes from the trunk and then hears the swishing sound of grass being splayed by feet.

"Sista Clark, we just thought we'd stop by and see how you was doing. Ain't seen you in church."

"Not for a while," a second voice joins in. "Six months or so."

Two women step into the clearing between the car and the house: Aberdeen Butler—carrying a basket of something with a gingham dish towel over it—and Hazel Sloan—holding a large paper bag with collard greens sprouting from the top.

"Been busy," Francine says, and tries to go around the women and head for the open door. The tomcat is mewling on the porch.

"Your baby sure is crying up a storm," Hazel Sloan says. "Girl, wasn't it?"

"Yes. Excuse me." Francine moves around the women and onto the porch.

"Lord's house misses you. Idle mind is . . . you know . . ."

"Here, cornbread to go with the collards. Greens right from Hazel's garden."

"They are taking over, greens all over the place." Hazel chuckles a little from the back of her throat. "I'm sure Joe Brown would cut this grass for you for a little bit of nothing."

"Getting kinda high, ain't it?"

"Baby's got good lungs. She alright?"

Francine heads for the door, but turns briefly to look at the women before she climbs the steps. The women eyeball one another and climb the steps behind her. She tries to stop them, but they are already inside.

Francine sighs loud enough to set off a warning. She thought country people at least had manners. She sets the bag of sweet potatoes down by the door. Coming up in someone's home. She scoops Mona up off the couch. Just inviting themselves in.

She bounces Mona and pats her back.

"Your house sure is pretty."

Aberdeen is spinning around slowly, looking in every direction.

Hazel Sloan focuses on the baby and the awkward way Francine Clark grips the child: around the chest, slumped like a dog, her head wagging.

"Won't you look at that precious little thing. Oh honey, you got to support her head."

"What's her name?" Aberdeen says, and scrunches her face up at the way Francine Clark is swaying the baby back and forth.

They listen for any hint in the name, look for features they can recognize in the tiny face.

"Oh honey, I can tell you ain't been around no babies. Let me hold her a minute. You got her twisted every which way."

A panic is rising in Francine's gut.

"Well ladies, thank you so much, but I really need to put her to sleep. She's got a little bit of colic." Her voice is strained and has the false lilt of her mother's. She has never been the type of woman to fight, but feels that low-class urge mounting in her now. She holds out her free arm and wiggles her hand as though shooing chickens.

"Colic? Best thing for colic is . . ."

"Ladies!"

"You should go get Minnie Mae Goode to blow smoke on her. That's the best cure. Worked on my young uns. Here let me . . ."

Aberdeen reaches for the baby.

"No."

The baby is quiet now, swaying beneath Francine Clark's arm, her eyes wide and focused. Hazel and Aberdeen have never seen anything like it—this way she's holding the baby, away from her, dangling like a . . .

"Well, I . . ."

"No!"

There is a tremble in Francine's voice. Her lip quivers. Something rolls through her hot and quick as thunder. Aberdeen Butler is so close that Francine can smell her breath and see the tiny hairs above her lip, the faded pink where her lipstick has been, flecks of red in the whites of her eyes. But what startles Francine most is Aberdeen's hand on her arm. First time she has been touched by somebody grown since being in the hospital. But that didn't count. This is the first time she's been touched since . . .

In her sleep, she thought the knock on the door was Sonny coming home from working the power lines. So she opened the door and buried herself into his chest. The smell was Sonny and not quite Sonny—sweet smell of man sweat. He kissed her long and hard, and yes, some fight rose up in her, but behind her closed eyes a cloudy vision of Sonny manifested itself and held her in the flesh. She refused to open her eyes, even when the voice that said "Now put your leg over here" didn't sound like Sonny at all. And when she was spent, he kissed up her thighs, and along the sweaty mounds of her fleshy stomach, and even in the creases beneath them and the insides of each of her flabby arms. "Beautiful," he said before he entered her gently, and even when she felt him spilling warm inside her, she didn't open her eyes. And when she felt the bed shift as he retreated from it, she kept her eyes closed tight and held on to her vision of Sonny. And he knelt (*Was he on one knee?*) and kissed her forehead, leaving behind a tiny wet spot that lingered there awhile after he had gone. And even when the kiss had dissipated into the cool air of the empty room, long after she heard the door close behind him and the scent they had made in the bed was all that remained, she still didn't open her eyes, and . . .

And now this thing whirs through her, and a pendulum swings itself back and forth. And sweat pours. And her eyes are on that spot between the collar bone and Aberdeen Butler's sweet neck, a harbor to cry into, and she can nearly feel Aberdeen Butler's garden-worked hand on her back and the warmth of their bodies touching. She can hear Aberdeen's soft voice whispering in her ear, sees all the women of Opulence gathered there in her living room, and her being folded into their circle. Minnie Mae Goode at the center, receiving her with full open arms. Aberdeen so close, sweet-voiced breath of a woman's assuring words . . .

She sees all this, hears it, nearly feels it before she raises her palm and slaps Aberdeen's face.

"Best you all get home," she says.

Aberdeen, who has stumbled backward from the blow and landed on the floor, scrambles to her feet.

"I said get out of my house!"

Francine screams so loud her voice turns hoarse and the loose skin beneath her chin shakes a little.

"We'll pray for you, Francine Clark," Hazel Sloan says. She places the greens and cornbread on the table. "And that young un too."

Mona begins to cry again. Aberdeen rushes toward Francine, but Hazel Sloan grabs her around the waist and pulls her toward the door.

"You better be glad you holding that baby. I'm a church-going woman, but all the devil ain't out of me yet."

"I'm gonna pray for you. Whole church gonna pray for you," Hazel Sloan says, pointing her finger before she grabs Aberdeen by the arm and is gone.

After she shuts the door, Francine retrieves the bottle warming on the stove. She jiggles the baby on the expanse of her belly until the child begins to calm. Francine Clark sways back and forth, then draws the warm nipple of the bottle to Mona's mouth. The tomcat comes out from behind the couch and begins to rub up against her legs. Must have rushed in when the door was open. Francine struggles back up off the couch.

"Filthy thing. Out you go, too."

She reopens the door and scoots the cat out with her foot. The grass looks like it has grown even more in the time she's been inside the house. She can see the top of Hazel Sloan's head. She's on tiptoe, trying to peep back through the living room window, but the shrubs are too high, and there is nothing more to see.

1972

Wild Birds on Easter Sunday.

Mona

One bird in one tree on Esther Street is warbling loudly.

Women stand on the limestone steps of Mission Creek Baptist Church wearing bright hats. It's Easter Sunday and cool, but the sun is shining a warm blanket over the congregation as they leave. The trees up on the knobs are tiny green guards in the distance.

At the edge of the churchyard, a little girl runs through the crowd and touches another little girl on the back. They sweat like boys through their Sunday dresses and then collapse to the ground giggling. Black faces nod parting greetings to one another, then disappear into dusty cars or strike out walking home.

The women in the hats begin to talk as the two little girls run across the yard again. There are no cupped-mouthed words or whispers among them. One of them places her hands on her hips and says, "Just look at that girl running wild."

"Wild sure enough," another says.

Then somebody adds something extra to get it all started.

"Can't tell who the daddy is by just looking, can you?"

The others groan from the backs of their throats in agreement.

"No telling."

"Ain't no telling who she done laid down with."

"Was somebody though, no doubt about that."

"Pretty little dark thing, though."

"Pretty ain't never got a body far for long."

"Born a bastard, die a whore."

They nod.

One of them clicks her tongue, another laughs as though they are talking about a grown woman and not a nine-year-old girl.

The words, somehow knowing their intended subject, float to Mona Clark across a swift spring wind, above the sound of the bird singing on Esther Street, past the last bit of chattering church folk now gathered across the grounds like a flock of sheep, and through the high-pitched squeals of playing children. Though she doesn't fully understand all of them, her ears catch every word. They climb their way up and rest on her sweaty dark neck. She stops playing and walks toward the women as if she will speak.

"Mona?" Yolanda calls out to her.

The women are so startled by the bold swagger of her bony ass, almost like a woman's walk, that they hush as she approaches.

Mona stops three feet shy of where the women stand, puts her hands where hips will one day grow, and stares at them. Not a girl's glance at all: she rests her eyes firmly on each of their disgusted faces long enough to make them squirm a bit in their skins, and then she laughs a throaty woman's laugh.

One of the women feels shivers go up her spine, but recovers long enough to clap her hands together and say, "Girl, go on somewhere! Get on back around the corner to your mama. Scat!"

And then they begin.

"Need to stay in a child's place."

"Evil, I reckon."

"Just like her mama for the world."

"Yolanda Goode you need to be watching the company you keep. Your Mama Minnie is a fine woman."

Musing over Tookie's troubles was once a pastime to women of a certain age in Opulence. Until now. They barely knew this Francine woman, who came way off from somewhere to marry Sonny Clark. Now look at what kind of child she's brought into this world.

"Somebody needs to whip this girl's little ass."

"Gonna whip the mama too?"

A solid hard thing forms in the pit of Mona Clark's gut, something she begins to live with, to almost embrace.

Girls. Ducks.
No Stars in the Sky.

Mona & Yolanda

It is late October, and the hills have colored up like beets and corn. The season balances itself between sweater weather and cold hard frost. Leaves flutter from the trees, and Joe Brown works in the driveway, his head buried underneath the hood of a car, his wrench tink-tinking against metal. Every once in a while, he lifts his head and watches Yolanda and Mona, sitting on the porch drinking pop in matching jeans and peasant blouses.

It is late in the afternoon when Yolanda says, "Daddy, we'll be back."

Joe Brown pops his head above the raised hood. "Be back before dark."

Boredom has bubbled up like sap, and Yolanda and Mona set off for a long walk. They walk away from town until they reach the Simpson place at the county line. They have heard about duck eggs near the Simpson pond.

"Billy Napier says they're big as chicken eggs and blue," Yolanda says. They have been to the Simpson place many times to pick the wild gooseberries that grow along the fencerow, to watch terrapins, to hear the kerplunk of frogs jumping into the pond.

It is the Simpsons' land, but the girls have never seen any of the Simpsons here. They see them in town. Nice white folks that their parents know. Mr. Simpson with that hawk-billed nose and Mrs. Simpson, plump and sweet-looking, her mouth curved like a bent teaspoon. They see narrow-tailed Obie Simpson—a stick of a boy—at school, but not here. They don't know Obie well, but like some of the other white boys in town, there is a certain way he looks at them that they don't like.

The land, the girls are convinced, is not Simpson land at all, just land, free for the coming and going of rabbits and birds and girls. On past visits they have seen traces of Simpson life: the car still steaming on a frosty Saturday morning, a hoe covered with fresh dirt leaning up against a woodpile, a fist-sized mound of marbles near the road. Once they heard Mrs. Simpson whistling, followed by the clack of the screen door, and then saw clothes flapping on the line. Sometimes when Yolanda and Mona see Obie Simpson at school, they jab each other in the ribs, so full of his secrets they could burst.

They enter the Simpson place through a hole in the barbed wire fence. Smoke curls out of the Simpson chimney in the distance. One silhouetted head, then another crosses the windows, but fear in any corner of their hearts is replaced by curiosity.

Squawking ducks grow louder as the girls come around the path. They delight in the tingling stench of pond water just a few yards ahead. Their spirits have an affinity for tadpoles swimming in slimy water buckets, the smell of gasoline, a tiny taste of mud pie. Duck eggs are this evening's obsession. They won't break them, they won't disturb them, just seeing them will be enough. Above them the sky is growing a dusky mauve, but the girls have not wavered in their determination.

They are only a few feet from the bank where they've

been told the treasure lies when Obie Simpson steps from behind a cedar thicket. His arms folded across his chest, trying to look older and more important than he will ever be, Obie stands with his legs cocked. His face is long, his mouth a straight slit of thin lips. One long shock of black hair curls over his left eye.

"What do y'all think you're doing?"

The girls, surprised, answer with the silent hunches of their shoulders and then look at each other.

"Minding our business," Mona says.

Obie Simpson, towering above them, looks like a sycamore, all trunk and long sinewy arms. He doesn't move from his spot, and says, "Looks like you trespassing to me."

When this new Obie Simpson, not the awkward, laughable one they see at school, moves toward them, a scream escapes from a small place beneath Yolanda's tongue. *Run!* She hears it as loudly as if it had been spoken aloud, and so she runs.

Mona stays still, and Obie Simpson grabs her arm. Mona's legs go, and she falls forward, barely bringing her other arm up in time to break the fall a little. On the ground, she tries to crawl away. She manages a small-voiced, "Obie Simpson, I ain't scared of you," but he grabs her legs and drags her toward him.

"Get off of me!" Mona says. The *me* lingers and struggles through the air before it bounces off the evergreens. Yolanda, realizing that Mona is not behind her, hears her hollering out and doubles back.

"Stop it!" Yolanda screams, and runs full force to try to knock Obie off of Mona. He blocks her with his elbow and throws her back toward the trees. After she lands, Yolanda looks back at Mona and Obie on the ground and scrambles behind a tree. She could jump in. She could run home to get her daddy. She could save Mona (maybe), but instead she just watches.

Obie Simpson sits straggle-legged on Mona's stomach, he brings his hand up as if he will strike her, but when his hand comes back down he slides it up under her shirt and grabs the skin where her breast will be. His chapped, field-worked hands scrape across her skin. He holds her there by her chest and presses all his weight down on her body.

"Get . . . off of . . . me."

Mona tries to get her leg high enough to kick him. Tries to bring her arms up to punch. He pulls his hand out from under her shirt to keep her from flailing her arms at him, reaches the other hand behind her neck and yanks her pony-tail.

Yolanda watches. Her legs won't move, but she thinks that if she wills it hard enough, Obie Simpson will let Mona go. If she wishes hard enough, her daddy will appear through the clearing, scare Obie off, and take them home.

"Bitch," Obie says. Then kisses Mona, his mouth so wide and awkward that his teeth clatter against hers. His tongue going in and out of her mouth like a lizard's, his breath rank with cigarettes and bad gums. Obie's eyes alternate between open and closed like a hoot owl.

"Stop . . . it," Mona tries to yell, turning her head from side to side, trying with everything she has to shake free.

Yolanda stays behind the tree.

Obie Simpson holds his forearm on Mona's chest while he inches her pants down. When her jeans rest below her hips, he wrestles with his own dungarees until he frees himself. Some-thing soft slaps against her legs, and somewhere in a moment when she should be most panicked, Mona sees a weakness rising in Obie's face, a slight vulnerable instant. She has never seen a boy's penis, and wants to see it. Even through these thoughts, she fights him. His penis grows hard, and she feels it slip into her spread thighs—not for long, just one time and only halfway, but she feels it—and a little, tiny feeling of glee replaces her fear and anger. Not because of the pleasure, because there is none, but because she recognizes something iniquitous. She becomes curious about this new thing, this certain kind of weakness she has not known that men and boys have until now. The tiniest grin forms behind her lips before she squirms loose, joins Yolanda, and runs across the fields toward the safety of home.

Obie Simpson runs after them, trying to hold his unzipped pants, and yells, "And don't come back. Damned black bitches."

By the time they reach a clearing and know Obie is not close behind them, Mona is adjusting her jeans, laughing as though nothing has happened.

This moment floats between them, a constant in the midst of their girlhood. This night comes back to each of them for the rest of their lives—in midday, at midnight, swooping down like a giant candle fly to a light, never letting up for long.

Mona thinks of Obie Simpson in the field whenever the story recycles its way back through her mind. She thinks of his hands, rough like sandpaper on her skin, his sour mouth on hers, his penis, her first, almost her first . . . the look on his face, that weakness in the tiny amber circle of his green eye. "He almost got me," she whispers.

Yolanda dreams of Obie Simpson. His white hands are weapons. She is drowning in the Simpsons' pond. A moldy stench like a cellar. Mona—pretty and younger, seven maybe, wearing her yellow Easter dress—Mona is drowning too, dying with a smile on her face. Her sunflowered chiffon dress billows up in the water like a sheet on a clothesline. She feels Mona's hand in hers. All she wants in that moment is her father to walk through the clearing, but Joe Brown is nowhere in sight. She and Mona are both disappearing. Down, down, down into murky water, Obie Simpson's hands on them. Smell of something rotting. Not a star in the sky.

1974

A Rock. A Stick.
A Hummingbird.

Mona & Yolanda

By July, things previously buried, dead, or forgotten are making their presence known, growing like choke weed, showing in the curves of thighs, the length of legs, clear on up to the fleshy pink of throats. Burgeoning hips. Breasts like tiny plums that just barely raise the fabric of blouses.

The girls are twelve, and though they know the landscape inch by inch, every time they walk they discover something new, something divine. A rock, a stick, a hummingbird. Cracks in the pavement that look like faces, wings of butterflies, each leaf fluttering in the summer breeze—even a red ant burrowing its way into dirt is a charm. Wild blackberries gleam fat and succulent on vines along fencerows, waiting to be plucked by girl hands.

They follow the road to its end, then turn the corner across the railroad tracks. They walk downtown, window shop at the dime store, then saunter back up Clover Road across Mission Creek Bridge and enter the Simpsons' land, where they make a discovery.

To most, it is just an empty field. Most would not notice this spot where the whirring sickle blade has been. This is the sort of place that adults would not notice at all. A field is just a field when you're full grown. Even the children, most of them, would dismiss it as nothing. The boys would kick at the grass until it disappeared, then be on their way to the creek for a swim. The girls would scream, "Oh look!" Maybe one among them with her child vision still intact would lie in the nest until the others pled with her, "Girl, hurry up."

But Yolanda and Mona, with only the slightest bit of adolescent hesitation, see happiness in the swoosh of long, dried blades of grass, arched and swirled like a giant bird's resting place.

Mona settles into the spot first, lies on her back, raises her spindly arms above her head, and plops her hands over her eyes. Except for the newly forming curves, Mona looks as she always has: straight hair, not much kink or curl, walnut hull skin smooth as butter, and that body straight up and down like a beanpole. Through her slightly spread fingers, she squints against the brightness of the sun.

Yolanda joins her. They lie in the quiet, grab handfuls of grass, and cover their bodies up to their chins. They each feel the prick and itch, but they cocoon themselves away in their nest, look up into the clouds, and marvel at the sky's distance from earth. They count birds and butterflies that pass above them. When it dawns on Mona that her mother doesn't know where she is, she smiles.

"Do you see it?" Yolanda asks. She keeps her eyes shut but bends her ear toward Mona.

"What?"

"The red? With your eyes closed you can see the red."

"You crazy."

"No. Look."

"Girl. You crazy."

"White women do this all the time," Mona says, throwing

her arm out in front of her, like a mother does when she means *You go on*.

"Do what?"

"Lay out in the sun to get black."

"They getting a suntan, Mona."

"Black, suntan, same thing. Some of them do it naked."

They giggle at the word *naked*, open up their eyes, and look at each other, then break into laughter again. They roll out of the nest and pick a large bouquet of the dandelion weeds that have already begun to poke above the freshly mown grass. They place the fluffy balls above their heads at the crest of their circle. They roll back into the straw palm, so close they almost touch. They lie on their sides with their faces toward each other like new lovers. Their lips come together and they kiss. Just a brief touching of lips, a kiss so light, so benign.

Years later, this moment comes wistfully back—the dewy feel of the lips, the milky smell of breath, the flutter of eyelashes touching for what must have been only milliseconds.

"You think I'm pretty?" Mona says, and rolls onto her back, the sunburnt weeds prickling through her blouse.

"Yeah. Me?"

"Yeah."

"I hope I'm pretty when I grow up."

"Me, too."

Yolanda doesn't say anything back, just looks up at the sky. They hold hands. They have never talked about Obie Simpson, but that day remains, like a full cup, always threatening to spill over. Yolanda closes her eyes again, trying to shut it out. She can feel her plaits coiling on the back of her head, drawing up in a pool of sweat. A sweat bee circles around her eye and so close to her ear that she can hear its buzzing.

"Dot Hill's having a baby," Mona says.

"Nuh uh. You lying."

"I could have a baby. I got my period," Mona says proudly, like she has won a prize. She says it with conviction, a tone that makes Yolanda feel extraordinarily young and silly.

Yolanda says nothing. They are quiet for awhile, just leaning into each other, their shoulders touching.

"I bleed."

"No you don't."

"I can have babies."

"Why you ain't told me?"

"Cause you don't need to know everything."

"I would of told you."

"Well I ain't you and you ain't me."

Yolanda can feel her foot shaking, a twitching in her toes. A sign she can come to count on most all her life.

"If I did it with a boy right now . . ."

Yolanda jolts up. She looks around to make sure no one hears before she responds. She clenches her teeth, tries to will the heat to stop rising, and spits out, "Mona, you so nasty."

"And you still got a baby pussy."

Yolanda slaps Mona before she even thinks about it.

Mona cups her cheek.

Yolanda's mouth gapes wide as a fish's. She's sorry, but this too has already become part of their story.

1976

Warming of Old Bones.
New Ways.
That Hurting Place.

Minnie Mae

Minnie Mae Goode declares, like she has every year from her front porch, when anybody will listen, that Dinner on the Grounds has been going on since slave times.

Another sweaty summer presents itself like a gift. Opulence is draped in red, white, and blue. Everyone is celebrating the two hundredth birthday of the country, and remnants of the Fourth of July parade have spread like a bicentennial plague, seeping beyond the borders of downtown well after the Fourth has come and gone; even Carter's Grocery still sports its huge awning flag, flopping patriotism and gas for seventy-six cents a gallon in the middle of July.

But beyond the bank, the dime store, the historic white-pillared homes with the American flags dancing in the wind, and the one-floor brick library just around a left-hand curve outside of downtown, before you reach the railroad tracks on one side or Mission Creek Bridge on the other side, another world is waiting. Every house is swarming with anticipation—the shingle-sided row house where Sweet Willie and Barnaby live, Old Man Lucien's bootleg house, Sandy Crawford's overly renovated redbrick ranch, the huge bi-level where the Goode clan resides, Francine Clark's little yellow house, and even below the hill, where the white people live. A thrill wriggles at the center of the hottest summer.

Women move their box fans from the bedroom to the kitchen window so they can cook. Corn pudding, candied yams, collards and kale, yeast rolls, mashed potatoes, and cole-slaw; sweet potato pie, blackberry cobbler, and peach up-side-down cake.

They carry their sweat rags between their breasts and pull them out to wipe salt from their brows. They have vowed never to do this again in the middle of July, but they always do. The heat and worry of the previous year is forgotten.

Sweet Willie brings a peck of Blue Lake runner beans to Francine Clark, and she shyly accepts them through a cracked door. Sandy Crawford has one of the children run a few of her prize-winning tomatoes to each home. Joe Brown goes to the icehouse in Lancaster for tubs of ice that sit on the back of Rooster Morrison's flatbed. Rooster is bringing pop. Old Man Barnaby collects five dollars from each family and picks up mutton, fryer hens, and a side of beef from the slaughterhouse up on Green Street. Ariel and a few volunteers clean the church until it's spick-and-span, even though the gathering will mostly be held outside. Reverend Townsend cuts the grass and buys twelve eight-gallon buckets of ice cream—chocolate, vanilla, and strawberry. It will nearly melt before anyone has a chance to serve or eat it.

Minnie Mae sits on her porch drinking lemonade and wipes her forehead with a handkerchief. She watches Yolanda and Mona saunter down the street, walking in unison like young girlfriends do, one set of long brown legs keeping perfect rhythm with the other. She notices the switch in their hips, dangly earrings, short shorts, Yolanda's hair standing out all over her head—an *Afro* they call it—and says, "Howdy-do la-dies?" over her glasses.

"Hey Mama Minnie," they say in unison, and wave up to her, giggle at themselves for echoing each other.

"Won't be long now," Minnie Mae whispers under her breath. *Hot-tailed*. She knows what comes after girls begin to fill out.

Minnie Mae dabs her head and fans her brow. She is rel-egated to porch-sitting duty now because of rheumatism in her legs and hands. In her days in her own kitchen, Henry dragged in the washtub of fresh mutton. The children ran through the house, excited about new loafers or a homemade dress. She baked her prize-winning blackberry cobbler, and felt the cool-ness of a cold glass of ice water easing down her throat. Even now, when she leans her head back into the rocker, she can see Tookie, her only girl, playing on the floor near the black iron cooking stove. It all comes back to her like a book, its pages being flipped by the breeze cooling against her hot skin.

Tookie trying out her new breasts in the mirror.

Minnie Mae giggling at her baby girl primping in the looking glass.

Boys coming around like old Pep in heat, wanting to bed her the first chance they could get.

But we didn't allow it in those times, not like they do now. I took a strap to that girl to try and keep her legs closed and her skirt tail down, but she crossed me every which way, turned bad on me.

Strikes a hurting place deep inside Minnie Mae's heart like a fresh, new wound. Most folks her age would have thought the stabbing pain was a heart attack, but she knows what it is: a broke heart.

In the distance, she sees tree-covered hills. It's always been a comfort to her to walk out on the porch and see the knobs. Reminds her of the old homeplace. So much has changed, but this land has always been here, steady and consistent, ready for whatever problems she sends up the hill. Goodness, the blue of the sky is a sight, still feels good to her old eyes. Air and sun reach down to her bones.

Way off down the street somewhere she hears a woman laughing. Minnie Mae recalls women up and down the gravel road not wanting their girls to come over and talk to Tookie, whose child skin by then spread out over her rounding woman's belly, tight as a drum.

After she had completed the chores, Tookie was just sitting in the chair peeling potatoes like she had been asked. Minnie Mae can't remember if it was Tookie's face that started it all or if it was that belly poking out like a swollen something. But even before she was fully aware of what she was doing, she started beating Tookie. She couldn't stop. Her grip around Henry's belt couldn't be broken, not by her boys, Butter and June, not by Tookie's screams, not even by Henry himself. She kept beating and beating, trying to beat Tookie back into good, looked down at red ridges rising up on her pregnant child's legs and back and kept beating. Tookie a mound of whipped flesh with big old sad eyes. She still remembers them old eyes. Was it fear or hate? *Ain't it a mama's job to protect?* Protect who? That's the question that rears its head now.

"Mama, stop! Mama, you going to hurt her!" Butter screamed.

June cried into his brother's shoulder and Butter kept pushing him away.

"Mae. Don't do nothing you can't live with." Henry talked to her like he was coaxing a jumper from the edge of a cliff.

But even when she remembered what old-time people said about slave-time beatings, she kept on.

When every other kind of talk failed, Henry finally left the sweet talk alone and jerked her up by the arm, his face turned mean, and in an instant she stood outside herself watching: Tookie coiled on the floor, her hands covering where the bastard child was taking shape, Henry demanding for her to stop, his grip tight as a belt around her arm, the boys' eyes red with tears.

As she thinks about it now, she thinks, *Selfish. Guess I was a selfish mama.* Wishing nobody could have ever said Minnie Mae Goode's girl turned bad. Tookie's the only girl she had, too.

Minnie Mae rocks in her chair.

She was glad that the baby was born at night, when nobody could see. Henry tried to persuade her to take Tookie to the colored hospital, but she wouldn't. Wanted Tookie to go through every single bit of suffering, her punishment for what she'd done.

After Tookie had accomplished the birthing by herself, Minnie Mae cleaned up Lucy and placed her on Tookie's chest. Then and only then did she reward Tookie with the gentle touch of her hand, pushing the matted, sweaty hair back from her forehead. Didn't say a word. No "It's going to be alright." No "I love you." Couldn't bring herself to say anything, though she knew deep down in her grieving-well that as a mother she should have provided some balm, like even the worst mama would have done. But most clearly Minnie Mae remembers Tookie's eyes, like a beat pup. Any pained creature always wears it about the eyes.

Minnie Mae looks down at her hands, holds them up to her face, remembers them straight and strong—holding crying

babies full of colic, rubbing liniment into tightened chests, ca-
ressing the back of Henry's head, cooking, cleaning. Funny
how these old hands could have given Tookie solace. She rests
them back in her lap.

She thinks of all her babies: the boys, Tookie, then the
grandbaby, now the great-grandbaby. She wonders if a girl
child will ever understand what she getting herself into when
her hips start to show.

"Not a blasted one," she mutters to herself. "Ain't nary
woman in this town got the sense that the good Lord gave
them. Opening up them legs anytime a feeling hits. Keep them
legs closed and everything be alright."

"Tookie," she had warned. "That girl's hips are out. You better
watch her."

But Tookie didn't do a thing. Shook her head, glued to
some spot in the yard out the window and said, "Mama, ain't
morning glories pretty?" And Minnie Mae's foretelling came
true. At eighteen, Lucy was two months along when she stood
up in white lace and baby's breath, but at least that time there
was a wedding in somebody's church. Nowadays seem like
they dropping like rabbits, them fatherless babies all over
creation.

"Here we are," Minnie Mae whispers to herself, or to
whoever might be listening from up on high. Tookie and Lucy
in the kitchen cooking for Dinner on the Grounds, and the
baby going off down the street in britches up to her bony tail,
her hips just a swinging.

But there is something about the girls' youngish bodies
that brings back the long ago firmness of her own skin, and the
weight of John Henry's large hand resting on the small of her
back as they flatfooted to the Victrola in her mama's sitting

room. The thoughts of her young self make her chuckle, which is just the sort of thing folks who walk by expect an old woman to do.

But those girls still worry her. Talking to the women does no good, so tomorrow she'll corner Joe Brown. She'll block his way out of the washroom after he's washed the car oil off his hands.

"Joe Brown," she'll whisper to her granddaughter's husband. "Keep watch on them gals. Especially that one they call Mona."

The Prodigal Uncles.
The Conk Story.
The Red Heat of Memory.

The Goodes & The Browns

Kee Kee, who has blossomed full into his body now, is standing shirtless, tinkering with his car, an apple-green Impala he's rebuilt from the motor out, when the uncles arrive Saturday afternoon.

Kee Kee likes it that he and his father are the only men in the house. He didn't so much as a boy, but now that he's nineteen, he relishes in opening a jar of something for his grandmother or helping his little sister reach the top parts of the kitchen cabinet. When the uncles come, they tilt the man-meter too far in the other direction.

He eyes the uncles descending in the shiny white Oldsmobile—a badass car, no doubt—but he keeps his head buried under the hood, and pretends like he never heard the smooth sound of the motor or the padded swoosh of doors closing.

June says, "Hey young man, look at you all grown, smelling your piss, I reckon." He steps toward Kee Kee with his arms held out, ready to give him the same bear grip he's been giving him all his life. Even though he's braced himself, even with pumping weights, Kee Kee still can't keep himself from being nearly toppled to the ground, just as he has not yet beat his father in a game of basketball.

"Hey Unc," he says.

"Hey boy," Butter says, patting Kee Kee on the shoulder. "Need a haircut, don't you?" He musses Kee Kee's Afro, which is as much affection as Butter is ever able to muster. His love seems to be buried so deep that there isn't much chance of seeing it.

"No Unc, the ladies like it just like this."

"What you know about some ladies?"

The uncles laugh on cue, like well-oiled machines, and ascend the steps into the house. That's another thing Kee Kee doesn't like: they laugh too much, seemingly when nothing is funny at all.

They hadn't waited on Kee Kee's response, but he certainly knows a thing or two about women. If the uncles made trips home more often, they would see proof, with the phone ringing all the time and the flock of girls always finding reasons to be near him. Some come from two counties over, with their eyes cutting at him, a few even bold enough to say what they've come for. Kee Kee shakes his head at his Uncle June's striped golf shirt and Uncle Butter's cowboy-cut blue jeans. They both look uncomfortable and out of place in their clothes, one too dressy and one too casual for their ages.

From her window, Yolanda has seen her uncles arrive and is relieved that they haven't brought her cousins with them. They always snarl their noses up at what she wears, how she styles her hair, and what she and her family eat. "Is that a real oxtail?" "Aren't you bored down here?" "Oh, you *do* have a TV?" or "Say that again, you sound so country." A part of Yolanda envies the city cousins for having access to the new Jackson Five albums first, long before they reach The Hub in Danville, that they have malls to shop in, that they can see movies in walk-in theatres and don't have to wait for them to come to the drive-in. But mostly she feels hate. She hates the way they act, like coming to Opulence is a punishment. Opulence is as good a place as any to live, better than some, better than most.

Tookie's brothers bring something young to life inside her. June, especially, makes her long to sit around with her mother and father like they used to, just the five of them, before everything changed. Hard for her to believe that June is full grown, even a bit gray headed, when she still remembers him peeing on her while she changed his diaper.

"You gave me a good spraying," she still says to him when the story makes its familiar way around the living room. Even now, with children of his own, she can make him mad by telling that story if she takes the notion. And he can do the same with her. Deep down, he's still the same soft-hearted boy. Butter hasn't changed much either, still mean as a snake and all his charms focused on their mother.

"Baby sister," he nods to her, his eyes still disapproving after all these years. "Looking good, looking good."

"Butter," she nods back, and reaches out to pat his arm.

"Tootie Fruity!" June shouts, and he and his big sister dance around the room. "How in the world are you, girl?" June pushes Tookie away from him to have a good look at her, then pulls her back into his arms. Settling right back into their child selves, June reaches down into a bag and watches Tookie's eyes light up. "I brought you something," he says.

Tookie can't help herself. She releases a girl giggle and cocks her head to the side, then cups both of her hands together like a ball and puts them over her mouth. "What is it?"

"Horehound candy, like we used to have as kids. Found it in Barboursville."

"Horehound candy, now that brings back some memories, don't it?"

By the time they have each taken a piece out of the bag, Kee Kee is coming through the front door, wiping his greasy hands on an old rag. Minnie Mae, Lucy, and Joe Brown have made their way into the big room.

"Old man," Joe Brown says to Butter. He grins and shakes his hand.

"Ain't too old to kick your butt, son," Butter winks at Lucy and gives her a hug.

"Lu-cy!" June screams, and hugs his niece, who is staring off toward the wall. "Man you better be treating this woman here right," he says to Joe Brown playfully. "And what's that mess on your son's head, looks like a rat's nest. Where's Yolanda?"

The men laugh and Kee Kee heads to the kitchen sink to wash his hands, not paying a bit of attention, even fluffing out one side of his Afro with the pick he always has in his back pocket, which starts up another round of laughter.

"Oh Lord, are my boys home?" Minnie Mae makes her grand entrance toward her beloved sons, pretending that the hint of lipstick and rouge is natural, and that she hasn't had her eyes beamed on the door for hours. "Didn't know y'all was here yet." She shuffles a bit more than usual, trying to look feeble, until she reaches them. "Both of y'all looking just like Henry. Y'all going to make your mama cry."

"Don't cry Mama," they say at the same time, and the three of them stand in the middle of the living room in a long triangular embrace.

"Something smells good," Butter says.

"Y'all might wake up in the morning and not have nothing to take to Dinner on the Grounds," June rubs his palms together.

"Have a seat. Y'all hungry?" Minnie Mae says, and turns

and shuffles toward the kitchen before either man has a chance to answer. Food is what she's always done best for the children.

Yolanda strolls into the room wearing a pink housecoat, making a grand appearance of her own, her hair in rollers, a mesh net spread over them.

"My goodness," June says, crinkling up his eyebrows in surprise. "Joe you got your shotgun ready? Looka here at this one."

"Don't need no gun," Kee Kee says, walking into the room, now clad in a sleeveless T-shirt. "These the only guns needed for any knuckleheads with bad ideas." He flexes his arm muscles and sends an echo of raucous laughter through the house. Joe Brown shakes his head at his son, covering his teeth with his hand to keep from laughing too hard.

"You ain't going to do nothing," June says.

"Watch and see if I don't. Let one of 'em come around and see."

"Come here and hug your uncles, Yolanda," Lucy says, her eyes darting back and forth from one family member to another. Yolanda does as her mother asks, taking her sweet time, like it's not something she prefers to be doing.

"Look at you all pretty," June says.

"Y'all got a nice-looking girl, there," Butter says to Joe and Lucy, but not to Yolanda. "The girls said to tell her hi." Yolanda plops down in a chair, which she knows is what her parents want her to do, though she and Kee Kee would both rather be in their rooms.

They're all jovial, at first, just like a reunited family should be. If a stranger wandered in, she would think it was perfectly fine, normal in fact, that the uncles' wives and children are not present and not missed. But by the time cake and sauce is served and eaten, and everyone has returned to the big room for conversation and a few laughs, just as always (it happens every time), things begin to twist.

Minnie Mae goes to her bed early. With all her children in her house, all she needs to make things whole is to go lie down and dream so that Henry can come to her. Nights like this make broken things fixed, places rarely touched are healed.

The rest of the family stays up late. In between checking on the dinner rolls and the hens in the oven, Tookie squeals in delight when the uncles tell stories on her. Even with the gray strands winding through her temples and the grimaces she makes when she stands up or turns around in her chair too fast, Tookie clearly holds the gladness of a child.

"Remember that time Tookie decided to give herself a conk?" Butter says, pointing and laughing so hard that the words barely spill out.

"A what, Uncle Butter?"

"A conk," June says, helping his brother out because he is laughing so hard tears are rolling down his cheeks. "Be something like a perm now. She wanted her hair slicked down like Smokey Robinson's."

Even Lucy, Joe, and the children have to laugh. Joe looks on amazed to see Tookie, who can be stoic at times, acting so silly. He's seen it when Butter and June have come home before, but the transformation surprises him each time.

"Your mama," Butter recovers and begins to tell the story straight to Lucy, "decided she was going to make up her own hair tonic, and somehow caught on that lye was the main ingredient, so she mailed off for some kind of recipe that was supposed to be the same recipe they'd used on Smoky Robinson's head, supposed to be some recipe that Madam C. J. Walker come up with. So Tookie gets to mixing up stuff and running around the house grabbing up this and that. And every once in a while you'd hear Mama or Daddy say, 'Tookie what you doing?' Tookie'd say, 'Aww nothing I'm a fixing my hair.' So me and June was back in the cut just a watching her cause she was always getting herself in some kind of hole that we'd have to help her up out of.

"So she's just a mixing and mixing, having some kind of dream that she was going to come out with white lady hair or at least Smoky Robinson hair." Then giggles get caught again down in Butter's throat, so June takes over the story.

"So she puts this God-awful mess a stuff on her head and Mama and Daddy is smelling all this and hearing all these jars and pots and pans and stuff clang together so they are still saying every so often, 'Tookie, what are you a doing in there?' And of course they were busy in the other room or out on the porch doing something. And Tookie's swatting me and Butter away like flies telling us to go on somewhere, but we won't leave because we want to know what the devil she's doing, so we just wait and wait, because Tookie had this history behind her of doing some crazy stuff now, so we both know something is coming that this is going to be a big one. So come to find out Mama and Daddy are on the porch stringing beans for canning and Mama's stringing and Daddy's breaking them up in this big ole water bucket filled clean up to the top with cold water. So anyway . . ."

Butter takes back over the story, and Tookie is sitting with her legs crossed and her foot is swinging nervously.

"So anyway, Tookie gets all this stuff on her head that stinks to the high heavens and she's got this stuff on her head about fifteen minutes when we look up and her skin is peeling all around here," Butter makes a sweep around his face from cheek, across the forehead, down to his other cheek in a half circle. "So me and June get to hollering for Mama and Daddy. And Tookie gets to running all through the house and all the way out back there past Mama and Daddy out into the yard hollering 'My head's a burning, my head's a burning!' So Mama and Daddy go chasing after her and finally me and June chase her down, then Daddy picks her up and brings her over and dumps her head down in that bucket of bean water and Tookie was just a squalling and then Mama started squalling about her mess a beans being ruined and later on Tookie said, 'I don't know which was the worse, being drown or being burnt to death.'" The brothers lean in on each other and laugh, tears running down both their faces like it's the funniest thing they've ever heard of in their lives. Tookie laughs too.

"'Nora Jean Goode,' Mama yelled at me, 'are you trying to kill yourself or kill us all,'" and Tookie laughs even harder after she's added her little bit, snorting and having a hard time catching her breath.

"Like a skinned chicken," June says and falls over again. Everybody laughs.

"Like a plucked, skinned chicken, with two feathers left," Butter adds and everybody laughs again.

Lucy slips out of the room to check on the hens in the oven and to see if the second batch of rolls is rising. She stares out the kitchen window into the dark, wishing something out there would come and take her away.

"Sure enough. I didn't have no hair all through here," Tookie motions around the sides of her hair. "Just a little bit left right up here at the top, but it was straight though, straight as a poker, so mama had to make me a little hat and I'd let my straight parts show up through that hat and I went on about my business like I was cute for the world."

And when all the juice is out of the conk story, one of the

three of them starts up on another one: the time Butter peed behind the stove before the bathroom got built and stunk up the whole house and got the whipping of his life; the time June almost drowned in creek water up to his knees; the boys chasing Tookie with a dead copperhead and made her so scared she wet her pants . . . Lifetimes of stories are stacked up one on top of the other in one night. But around ten o'clock, the laughing stops.

Lucy has just returned from the kitchen and squeezed back into her place beside Joe. "Everything's done Mama, I cut it off. We'll put the rolls on come the morning."

"I remember when your mama had you," June says to Lucy before he's even thought about it. "You sure was a lot cuter than you are now." He has tried to recover, and even got a little chuckle out of Lucy's kids, but the levity is draining quickly. Lucy takes Joe's hand and squeezes it.

"Me and June's been wanting to talk to y'all," Butter starts out. He eyes the kids like he thinks they should go to bed, but they don't. Yolanda remains in her spot beside her parents on the couch, now curled into her father's side, the uncles are on the love seat, and Kee Kee is sprawled on the floor, half paying attention and half watching the TV, which is turned down low, his other ear bent toward the wishful ringing of the phone.

Butter leans back in the chair, clearing his throat, rubbing his hands through what hair he has left. "Mother's getting up in age . . ." The regular Goodes (Browns too) lean forward, steadying themselves against the changing wind they can detect in the room, going from warm to cool, damn near ice cold. Lucy folds her arms and rubs them against the goose bumps. ". . . and I know you all don't want to start thinking about all this, neither do I, but anyone with common sense knows she doesn't have long for this world." Butter has gone from talking proper to his regular country self and back to proper again. Joe Brown notices.

"Just stop, Butter," Tookie puts her hand up in the air and bends her head toward her lap, where her skirt tail is bunched up too high, showing her stocking.

"Hold on Tookie, listen to what Butter's got to say a minute."

Tookie rolls her eyes at June, feels her face and shoulders grow hot with fury. Joe Brown puts his arm around Lucy and rubs the back of Yolanda's head. He realizes this isn't his family business, and he's trying to stay out of it. Lucy's listless stare still makes his stomach flop if he watches her too long.

"It ain't right for nobody to be talking about Mama dying and her just right down the hallway living right on!" If Tookie really was a girl again, she would punch each of her brothers in the belly and then run off to her own room. She crosses her arms and turns her head toward the kitchen with a seriousness about her that helps empty the last bits of sunshine out of the living room.

"What I'm trying to say, Tookie, is you ain't young. I ain't young, hell I'm sixty years old. Hell, even Lucy and Joe ain't young no more, and ain't nobody going have the money to take care of Mama when it comes to that point. So we better be thinking about it all now."

"I don't want to talk about anything that involves Mama Minnie dying," Lucy says, and tries to rise up and leave.

"It's okay, Lucy. You got the same right to be here as any of the rest of us," Joe Brown whispers, so she settles in. For a second Joe Brown thinks that if Kee Kee climbed up and joined them, then there they'd be, all the Browns leaning into each other like Lincoln Logs, side by side, sticking out all this crazy talk together.

"Just hear the man out," June says, louder than he should, and everyone gets quiet, shocked that he would make such a show of himself.

"All I'm saying is that families get themselves into this situation all the time when they don't plan. We'll be a whole lot better off if we start making plans. Do it right now before worse comes to worst."

"Unc, what the hell you talking about?"

He's a grown man by most standards, but to everyone in the room, most especially Butter, Kee Kee is a child to be contained to a child's place.

"Boy, this ain't none of your business."

"Why ain't it?"

"Cause it ain't."

"Butter, don't talk to the boy like that."

"Like what? It ain't none of his damn business. Kids ought to be in bed."

"How the hell you going tell me what my kids need to be doing?"

"And you ain't in the family, neither, Joe. You ain't blood."

Joe Brown catches his teenage self slipping back. No surprise that an insult to his family would get his back up, but what does surprise Joe is that he's bracing himself for a fist-fight if need be. His fist is balled up by his side before he can even stop himself.

"Butter, you getting out of line." June is always good at cooling down hot situations. Usually. "We was thinking that we ought to sell the homeplace."

"No," Yolanda is in it now. "No, you can't."

"Y'all have lost your natural damn minds. If Mama knew y'all was in here talking about this she'd . . ."

"Going to have to happen sooner or later. I just thought

we could be civilized about this, but I see that no one here has the sagacity to handle reality."

"*Sagacity* . . . your . . . ass, Butter. You and your big-ass words can go on back to Lexington." Tookie's voice is shaking, and with that she pulls herself up to her feet, steadies her knees, and heads to bed. "And take your brother with you. He's so far up your ass I guess you couldn't help but take him right on along."

June playfully says goodnight to his sister, trying to bring just a bit of joy back into the room, but Tookie just nods her head. It suddenly feels cold to June. He rubs his arms.

All Tookie can think of is that time when Lucy was little and almost drowned in Mission Creek, how she couldn't make her knees work right back then, even when she was a much younger woman. She deliberately turns her head away from June, from Butter too.

"Good night," she says to Kee Kee and then to Yolanda, sweetening her voice back up for her grandchildren. She pats Joe Brown's arm, which makes his fist loosen, kisses Lucy on the cheek, then slowly heads down the hallway to bed. It isn't until she's in the hallway that she realizes how much her knees are hurting, how this conversation has taken her from girl to old woman so quick . . . She squeezes the back of her neck—she feels a pain there too.

Joe Brown calls good night after her.

Then the Brown family goes to bed, not saying goodnight or anything else to Butter and June. Morning will be dry and cold compared to the red heat of memory that filled the room earlier in the evening.

Butter and June sit on the love seat long past midnight. June sucks in a deep breath and lets it out, "Shoo."

"I couldn't live here back home for nothing," Butter says, looking all around the house.

"I've thought about it, maybe when I retire."

"You're kidding, right?"

"No, I've thought about it. Probably couldn't get Frieda and the kids to do it though, moving from Cincinnati to Lexington was hard enough on them. Maybe when all the kids are up and out." June gets up and starts taking the pillows off the couch to pull it out into a bed.

"Couldn't do it for the world. Ain't nothing here for me except Mama."

June can't fully understand Butter, and he can't stand up to him even now. This is his big brother after all. But he hates that he's made Tookie so mad at him, even though he's still convinced Butter has a point.

" . . . Mama and the rest of them too of course," Butter adds. "But family's going to be family wherever they're at."

"Ahh, I don't know," June says. "Past always going to be there. Ain't no getting away from it."

"Yep, but you ain't got to wallow in it and you ain't got to die in it."

"You go on and take this bed," June says as he finishes putting the sheet on the mattress. "I'm going to make me a pallet over here by the register, you being old and all, your back and all." He shoots Butter a grin.

"You're rotten to the core," Butter says back, and throws a pillow at June. "I ain't in bad enough shape not to whip you."

"You better watch it, don't want your mama have to come in here and save you." One last chuckle between them for the night.

This is good, June thinks to himself, these moments. They both live in Lexington, but they don't get together often enough. Have their own lives. A part of June would love to climb in bed next to his brother, like they used to, but he has sense to know grown men don't do that. He pulls enough blankets and pillows from the hall closet to cushion the floor. Life sure is changing. Mama is looking older, Lucy's kids all grown up. The house looking a little more worn. Usually Lucy and Joe give up their bed and sleep with Yolanda, but after the talk there had been none of that tonight. Feels good to be home though, and Dinner on the Grounds is tomorrow. That should lighten things up, and then they'll say goodbye.

Dinner on the Grounds.

The next day at the church, Joe Brown watches cars line up along both sides of the street. Not just the normal neighborhood cars, the newest of which are at least two or three years old, but brand new cars that gleam in the sunlight and still smell car-lot fresh and sport black glistening tires that haven't seen much dirt yet.

Two church buses full of out-of-towners pull into the lot, and a long, silver charter bus with air conditioning and a bathroom on board careens along the blacktop until it comes to a high-profile stop right in front of the church like a limousine. Fifty-five strangers from Atlanta strut off the silver steps: a guest choir. People mill in the street. All of Opulence's wayward children, even those who live as far off as Texas or California, show up talking city talk and driving long, shiny black Cadillacs and red sports cars. They bring exotic gifts for their relatives—silver trays for chitterlings and fried potatoes and crystal goblets for Kool-aid and sweet iced tea. The mothers and grandmothers say, "Thank you, baby," and will wait for the out-of-towners to leave before placing the items in the attic with the other strange things their kin have brought home. They bring candy that they claim is the best of the best, which

makes children tear up their faces and spit out the bitter chocolate and head to Carter's Grocery for the Laffy Taffy and
sweet-tasting chocolate they're used to. They bring young
women expensive bubble bath with aromas so foul and foreign
that they give it to their children to wash their dolls' hair, or
give it to the boys to wash the dogs in. All this, of course, after
the courteous "Thank you" and polite "That smells so good."

Children are dressed for church, but run through grass
with wild abandon. Little boys avoid their mothers' glares
when brown stains appear on the knees of their best dress
pants and their ties flap crookedly in the wind. Mothers notice
aloud that the press and curls they had set off with blue, pink,
and white ribbons have wilted with girls' sweat in the July
heat. Little girls stare down at the ground, then run back to
play. Toddling children, who were told over and over how
handsome or pretty they are before they left their homes, cry
when they get ice cream on their pants or tear a hole in the
knee of their white tights or scuff their patent leather shoes.

Old women beam smiles under Sunday hats when a lad
from Lancaster or Harrodsburg says loud enough for all to
hear, "I drove all the way from Lexington just for a taste of
Miss Christine's buttermilk pie." And the young man saunters
up to the table where Miss Christine stands proudly behind
her pies, puts his hands up in the air, and says, "Thank the
Lord and Jesus there's still some left." Each of the women, if
they are worth their salt, has suitors, not in search of their
womanly wiles, but in search of some delicacy that they only
taste once a year at this time.

Younger single women fill their plates and coyly peep
through sunglasses, sometimes nudging one another when a
single man walks into the churchyard. Many a match is made
during Dinner on the Grounds. It has always been this way,

and it has always been tradition to buy a special Dinner on the Grounds dress or to get one made.

So here they are, the seeker women, lined up like blossoms in a flowerbed, in their lilac and white, daffodil yellow and sherbet orange. Their lace and ruffles and Peter Pan collars. Some outfits are accompanied by gloves. Some with hats. Some of the sisters have elaborate hairdos that sit up like rooster crowns, pomaded and glistening in the Opulence sun. And every pair of succulent, young, waiting lips is painted the perfect shade to match not only what the woman is wearing, but also the hue of mahogany or honey or oak that is her skin. They are ladies in waiting, talking in small groups, eating at picnic tables, twisting up church steps, or stepping elegant Jackie-O steps like they are on a runway, just in case there is a man in the crowd who is husband material.

Brothers are dressed to the nines, too. Brothers who might attend church every Sunday, brothers only a few hours from the bootleg house or the dance hall, waltzing into the churchyard with their gabardines and their pinstripes and their solid churchly blacks and browns, suited down and ready to feast on food and women. Brothers who are as handsome as Billy D. Williams, some carrying the heaviest scent of cologne on their neck bones and the slightest hint of liquor on their breath (nothing that a stick of mint gum or a peppermint stick won't mask, as long as they avoid their grandmothers long enough to sober up). There is no missing this day for any reason.

The occasional sister has gone too far, and worn a dress that is almost too revealing for the dance hall, let alone Dinner on the Grounds. And there is always at least one brother who shows up wearing some flashy outfit, red or green or purple, and Jheri Curl juice on his shirt collar and gold teeth flashing in the sunlight. But what Dinner on the Grounds is complete without everybody. Then the regulars wouldn't have as much to talk about. And talk they do.

Joe Brown stands with his arms folded and watches all of this, as he has since moving here.

Minnie Mae fans herself in the shade and purses her red lips together. Tookie stands by her mother, places her hands on the belt of her new lemon-yellow dress, and shakes her head.

"Look at that hussy on the Lord's ground," Minnie Mae says, fanning herself faster and leaning her head back in her chair.

"Good Lord," Tookie says, as though she has forgotten what they've always thought of *her*. If she let herself speak, there's a lifetime of words that would fall right out, so she doesn't say much.

The other old women join them, shaming the woman into being self-conscious enough to try and pull up her dress in the front, even though it is an impossible task.

But the brother, the Jheri-curled brother, he is too brazen, too deep into believing in his own good looks to even acknowledge the stares he receives as anything but praise. He steps onto the church grounds with a dip in his step and takes in every glance, every stare like a compliment.

Another brother hobbles in on crutches and sports a black eye from a late-night brawl. Two women, seen having words over a man, come in on opposite sides of the church field. They roll their eyes and proceed into the church like they have some sense, a little to everyone's surprise—but there has still never been an incident in all these years, not in the Lord's house.

There are more hugs during Dinner on the Grounds than at any wedding or funeral. Classmates old, fat, and gray hug each other and tell stories of when they played together in first grade, when they used to be neighbors, when they were bony or short or had lots of black hair. Butter and June are right in the middle, shaking hands like politicians, laughing like hyenas.

"Negro, where you been? We ain't seen you since Heck was a pup."

"How's your mama? Better yet how's your sister? If I wasn't married I'd look her up."

Yolanda thinks they are embarrassing, and she still hasn't forgotten the talk last night about Mama Minnie being ready to die, so she avoids the uncles as best she can.

Old lovers hug while their spouses nod and glance approvingly; through a sixty-second embrace they reminisce every moment they ever spent together. Brothers and sisters hug, remembering their dead parents or siblings or friends. Some people hug because they just met, and it is good to see everyone together one more time. Strange or familiar, it doesn't matter. Even the white folks who come—whether they are part of the community and just stopped by to say hello, or come from town and know that there is an abundance of good food— receive hugs. The talk will come later.

"Do you remember that old white man with the blue hat that was at Dinner on the Grounds? That was Mr. Floyd, Bert Floyd's son. Would steal from you just as soon as look at you."

Or

"Did you see that white woman from up in Lancaster? Came just to try and find her a black man, I bet."

Or

"The Carters stopped by Dinner on the Grounds this year. They're the nicest white folks I ever did see."

But before the talk, they all get hugs, unless there is a clear reason for them not to. Like Nelson Burton. Nelson always comes to Dinner on the Grounds, pushing his wheelchair through gravel and grass to sell his bars of candy. Word is he got hurt in a coal mine somewhere up in the mountains. Near Harlan, some say. Nobody hugs Nelson—not because he is white, not because he is crippled, but because he smells. The old people say, "The boy ain't seen water since the mine got hold of him." But everyone who can buys one of his melting candy bars, then throws it out for the ants and the dogs after he leaves. Nobody treats Nelson mean, except the one child who gets out of hand and dances around his wheelchair and taunts him, but that child is quickly pulled aside and spanked because that isn't any way to act.

Though Nelson Burton isn't greeted with a hug, one of the older men bends over, takes Nelson's withered hand, and thanks him for coming. This makes the children cringe, but any child of Opulence knows it is the right thing to do, even if their guts churn at the thought of grabbing Nelson's shriveled nub in theirs and shaking it.

This is a day of celebration, but also one of the finest days to praise God. The true church-goers and some of the pretenders enter the church and listen to Reverend Townsend's sermon and the sermon of the guest minister, and hear the three guest choirs sing before they make their way back outside to eat. Not that some aren't salivating at the mouth or nudging each other or wiggling in their seats because they're hungry, but they still do what they think is right and wait.

The true believers amen themselves into hoarseness, and cry with joy when a woman in one of the guest choirs hits a note so high they know she must be one of God's angels, sent to them for this day. And their faces are pure bliss when, during Reverend Townsend's sermon, two out-of-towners get the spirit and shout so hard they have to be restrained. And Reverend Townsend beams with pride and winks at his fiancée, Ariel, when the guest minister says what a fine church and congregation Reverend Townsend has.

Yolanda and Mona witness that wink and giggle, even though they are sitting in the back of the church, which is what they do. They notice every single thing that happens in Opulence, and they soak up the way grown people carry on. They watch couples hold hands and loop arms, even if they were fighting the week before.

Many a marriage has begun at Dinner on the Grounds, and many a union has been broken there too, when strange eyes meet across the churchyard. Some light clicks on in the eyes of a woman and a man. The girls have seen the two sneaking away from one or the other's house a week later, acting upon some affection sparked on that day. They've watched strange men and women driving up Hickory Grove a month after Dinner on the Grounds, searching for the love they thought they found that Sunday, or in search of the mate who has discovered someone new and gone astray. They watch even the plainest of women transform themselves for Dinner on the Grounds in hopes of catching flame to a transformed man, even if that man was one of the drunks, one of the ne'er-do-wellers, or out of a job. And the men, even the ones who are ugly as sin, the ones without jobs, the ones who are in the middle of bitter divorces, the ones with no teeth, sometimes leave Dinner on the Grounds with a woman on their arm.

Yolanda and Mona watch it all, and learn their lessons well.

The Homeplace.

In late August, when Minnie Mae and her sons arrive at the homeplace, the country feels like it's settling down to rest for the night. A slight breeze rustles the trees, and sounds grow up and out around them until the hundreds of creatures large and small become one loud voice. It is as if the night has taken up the voices of the Goode kin long past, and even Butter and June, with their new city ways, have to listen.

The old house leans and the porch sags; this same old house where Minnie Mae and Henry lived as a young couple. Every spring, the boys come to help Minnie Mae clean up the yard and plant the early garden. In fall, they come help her rake the leaves. Though nobody lives there now, she insists on sweeping the dirt around the back porch into a series of swirling patterns and pinching back the hens and chickens growing in a big white tub on a stump. Butter leans on the handle of a grubbing hoe and June stands holding a clump of weeds, the fresh white roots reaching down toward the ground.

"This is y'all's what-for," Minnie Mae says, placing one hand on her hip and the other one spreading far and wide from one edge of the knob across the creek to the other side. The moon is out and the farm is glowing behind her. "All this," she says, "been up under your people's feet since slave times. My mama and daddy worked this land, and their mama and daddy before them.

"Old Man Hezekiah started all this. Back in 1878, just one hundred years after Daniel Boone blazed a bloody trail through here, killing every Indian he saw, Old Man Hezekiah (he was freed from Virginia) paid one hundred and fifty-six dollars for eight acres of land right here. Old-time people always said that Old Hezekiah was a tree of a man, a master carpenter. They say he got fighting mad when white folks called this 'nigger town' so he put up a sign twenty foot long across the road here saying this place was to be called *Opulence*. Course a lot of people around here then didn't know what that meant, but the old-time people say he cut the sign out of the finest of woods and carved elk, bison, foxes, and birds all over it, and then wrote *Opulence* as delicate as a teacher's cursive with a chisel. Been Opulence ever since.

"It's true.

"There's a picture of him that hangs on a bent nail down at the library. Down below that picture there is a cigarette lighter made of pure silver, a pearl-handled pistol, and a Bible, all sitting on a little oak table. There are three dry-rotted blue dresses with shiny brass buttons, said to have been worn by his wife and two daughters; a wooden rattle, a piece of shorn leather strung through it end to end; and the second son's first blanket, torn from his mother's skirt tail; and over in the corners, behind glass, and on drop leaf tables are a rusted harness, blue Mason jars with healing salve (according to Arnetta Berry), a boar-haired brush and wooden comb, a child's whirly top, and a black leather satchel with a symbol on it shaped like a heart, said to have been brought all the way over from across the waters. Arnetta guards it all like it was made of Fort Knox gold. She's somewhere kin to y'all. You should go by and see it yourself. Me and your daddy moved to town, but we came down here and worked this land too. All y'all was raised up on money the tobacco brought in and the garden food we put on the table. Over that ridge there is a graveyard, a whole village of our folks over there. Knew all their names when I was a girl, but some of them done left my mind now. Show your respect once in a while. You boys played over there in them fields when you was little."

Minnie Mae loops her arms around the waists of her boys, fingers from one hand rung through the loops of Butter's belt loops, the other resting on June's back.

"This going to be y'all's and Tookie's one day. Pap stood right there out by that well and said that's all a man needs is some little piece of rich earth and a good woman. Reckon he got what he needed in your grandmother. And she got what she needed in him." Minnie Mae shifts her hips to ease the aching through her hipbone. Looks from one of her boys to the next. "I don't know nothing about being a man. Can't say I've raised you up to be good men, but I've done the best I can. I do know what a good man is. Your daddy was a good man. My daddy was a good man. Good man's more than breath and britches. Man has gumption. Woman, too. Woman's got to have more gumption than a man sometimes. Woman goes through more things and then got to help the man bear his burdens . . ."

Butter breaks his mother's grip. "Mama, I don't see why you don't sell this old place. None of us set to be farmers. We all got our own lives. Good lives. It's just setting here growing weeds. The house is falling in . . ." He places his hand on her shoulder. "You know you're getting too old to keep putting in a garden, and look at the house ain't nothing much left but firewood."

"Hush your bad mouth. Can't even see yourself when you feasting your eyes right in the looking glass. Hush your ignorant mouth. This ain't about no grade a wood on no house."

"Mama, Butter's right." June looks down toward the ground and kicks at the dust. Deep down he knows his mother is the freight train gaining steam that she's always been, not much meek and mild about her, even now.

"Not one, but two full-grown damn fools. Take me on back home. Can't see yesterday then you don't know what's coming your way tomorrow. Let's get going. Plumb damn ignorant. You are a shame before God, your daddy, and all your people."

Again the boys, who have somehow, without Minnie Mae noticing, turned into men—some kind of men—stare at their mother as though an old folks' home would suit her fine, with a patronizing glint in their eyes usually reserved for young children who have gotten out of line.

She is angry at them both, but Minnie Mae's heart still dances with glee when her boys come home. And even though they're adults with grown children, she still dotes on them and fixes blackberry cobbler for Butter and corn pudding for June, even when her legs are hurting her bad.

"Your daddy spit you right out," she says to Butter each time he steps his long legs from whatever new car he has purchased, and she rubs up and down his arms like they're the arms of her Henry, long dead. And she grabs Juniper by the jaws and kisses each of his cheeks like a mother would a boy of five. And of course she loves the grandchildren, even if they are a strange lot. The wives are insignificant. Don't have the same sweetness about them that the son-in-law has. Joe Brown, now that's a different story, he's like a third son, one without blood, but with a bushel of sense.

But when it comes to June and Butter, once the initial hugs are made, the general "How are yous?" delivered; once dinner has been served and eaten; then foreigners step into the bodies of Minnie Mae's babies. She's come to prefer not the boys themselves, but the memories they trigger. When the past has filled her mind completely, a somber silence sets in and they are free to get on back to where they came from.

When they get back to Opulence from the homeplace, Minnie Mae insists that the boys head on back to the city so they won't be driving home too late in the dark. She doesn't beg them back into the house for pie or ask them to spend one more night.

Long after Minnie Mae has watched the taillights of her sons' cars disappear into the dark, she stands on the porch and scrapes the mud off her boots. Joe Brown hears the stick hitting against the wood and comes out to join her on the porch. He invites her to sit down in the rocker, then places his jacket across her lap. He lifts her boots up on his knee and scrapes the remaining mud. He says nothing. Minnie Mae doesn't say anything either, but stares out into the night like she's focused on the bark of one lone tree out there in the yard. But she does let out a long sigh when she lifts and offers her hurting leg and its heavy boot to her son-in-law.

Moonlight pours across the porch like a big bowl of creamy soup. Minnie Mae relaxes into the chair and nods off to sleep. A cat yowls like it's hurt somewhere down the street, and a breeze takes up the leaves. Somehow Joe had been thinking that maybe if Butter and June went down to the homeplace, everything would fall into place and they'd understand what it all meant. But he can tell by Mama Minnie's posture that nothing good has happened on this night.

He is reminded of the time he and the women stopped for a picnic one summer down at the homeplace near Mission

Creek. Minnie Mae and Tookie packed cold sandwiches and fruit wrapped in tinfoil, and they put a few cans of pop in a rusty blue cooler in the trunk of the car. They spread a couple of old quilts on the ground and watched a flock of geese fly over them . . . Lucy sat quietly and dipped her hands in the creek, scooping up palms of water then letting it trickle through her slender fingers. Tookie cradled Kee Kee in her lap and rubbed her fingers through his hair until he fell asleep across her like a kitten. This was long before Yolanda was born. Minnie Mae hovered over the food just like she was at a stove back at the house. She looked peaceful, but she had been talking about Mr. Henry and her boys all day long.

From where they had positioned themselves, they could see the roofs of the barn and the old homeplace. The sun was streaming down and spreading yellow on everything like a painting he had seen once. Right now, he can't remember what the occasion was. But he recalls the purest feeling of happiness that washed over him in those moments.

Joe looks over at Minnie Mae, her silver head dipping toward her chin, and smiles. Her head bobs down hard and she suddenly wakes, a little embarrassed.

"Law me," she says. "Bet I was snoring." She wipes the side of her mouth with the back of her hand.

Joe squeezes her shoulder and then opens the front door where they see the entire family readying for supper. "Let's get you in the house Mama Minnie," he says. "You gone catch a chill out here."

1977

That One Thing Her Mother Warned Her About.

Mona

The night after her first encounter with Mouse, Mona stretches out in bed and thinks of him. She still throbs between her legs. It's pain mostly, where Mouse's fingers have been, but she finds a great thrill in the secrecy of it all, the feeling that had begun with Obie Simpson that day in the woods and maybe even before then if she thinks about it hard enough. It excites her that she has moved a step closer to that reticent thing that her mother has warned her about. Sex? No one has ever really talked about it, so it must be special. And all this waiting. For what?

So she lies there in the dark, the moon showing its brightness through the window, listening to a dog howling in someone's backyard, and thinks of how Mouse pulled her panties down as though he had done it hundreds of times, and jabbed his fingers inside her. Then he put her hand on his privates—a small, gristly thing, like a tiny chicken neck ready for frying. She giggles at first, then laughs, shaking the calm in Francine's house.

Francine rouses up from her own bed and speaks across the hallway. "Girl, have you lost your good mind?"

And the knowing, swelling inside Mona makes her laugh hard and loud, disturbing her mother's peace before she finally responds with, "Yes, ma'am, good night."

1978

The Birthday Dinner.
First Sign.

Mona

It's December, and Mona has lost her tongue again inside the Goode house, sitting at their dining table. She loves the clutter and the vastness of the house and all the people and things that fill it up. A large stash of brown paper and plastic bags nest underneath the kitchen sink alongside empty Mason jars. There is always a container for june bugs and frogs and candle flies, always a bag to carry books and clothes and hair barrettes and doll clothes back and forth, always a cake cooling on the stove and somebody saying something.

"How's your mama?" Lucy eyes Mona while she pours a helping of soup into the girl's bowl. "This enough?"

"Yes, ma'am, that's good," Mona answers with her eyes lowered toward the table. "Mama's fine," she adds.

"Bless her heart."

Tookie sips her iced tea and breathes so heavy through her nose that everyone in the room can hear the air squeezing in and out of her, making a whistling wind noise. But nobody says anything about it.

Mona has been raised to keep her mouth closed, to let all the words in the world stack in her throat. So she doesn't say much, only responds to the questions.

Joe Brown and Kee Kee shake their heads at the women.

Kee Kee crumbles his cornbread into his bowl. Joe Brown drinks his water down in loud gulps.

"Does your mama know you left the house in that skirt up to your hind end?"

"Mama Minnie!" Yolanda says with an uncomfortable smile.

"Mama, Lord have mercy!"

Lucy wiggles uncomfortably in her chair, picks at her food.

Joe Brown grabs his son's shoulder in a knowing gesture, as if to ask, "Ain't women something else?"

"Well it's cold, and the child ain't got no clothes on except that strip of skirt and them boots."

"Well, so how's school, Mona?"

"Fine, Mr. Brown."

Joe Brown knows what the women in his family think about this girl, and has heard the things that the whole town has said about her mother, but he admires her guilelessness. How she would fight back if she was backed up in a corner by the women in this town. He can't say he lusts after her like some of the grown men do—he's heard them talk too—but something about the fire in her reminds him of girls from his own childhood: girls who could be polite like they were raised to be, but who were also sometimes sharp tongued, even with adults. He scrapes his spoon through his beans and thinks of those back-talking girls from his boyhood.

"Glad to hear you doing good," he says.

"Mona, you ready to go up to my room?" Yolanda pushes herself from the table.

"Not 'til that food is gone away from here."

"Somebody get the pie."

"Somebody needs to wash them dishes, is what somebody

needs to do. I'm too old to be washing them and cleaning up after people all the time."

"Mama, we'll get the dishes later," says Tookie. "Lucy, bring that girl's pie on in here."

"A girl can't turn sixteen and not have dessert," Joe Brown says.

Mona watches Kee Kee, flitting her eyelids like jar flies.

Kee Kee gulps his tea, takes another bite of cornbread.

Tookie has made Mona a rhubarb pie. It was Lucy who sunk the candy HAPPY BIRTHDAY letters into it and poked sixteen pastel-colored candles into the center, causing the crust to crack.

Mona watches Joe Brown. She imagines herself at his table every night, ridding herself of the loneliness that she feels with her own mother. *Father, father, father,* she thinks, and stares at him, his wide jaw, his large scarred hands.

She grins so wide that Joe Brown laughs and says, "What is it, Mona?"

To which she replies, "Thank you all, that's all."

Minnie Mae says, "Poor child."

Yolanda cuts her eyes at Mama Minnie, but does it shyly so she doesn't get accused of sassing back. Some things can't be excused away by old age. Mona looks at each of them, claiming each member of Yolanda's family as her own, especially the Brown men.

When her family gathers around Mona's pie and sings the birthday song, Yolanda suppresses disappointment. She doesn't know exactly why it's there, but she feels it. She watches her father and her brother smiling at Mona while they eat their pie. This is probably the first sign as to how things will go.

Flapping Wings. Nightjar. The Story of a Scar.

Mona & Yolanda

"I don't want my hair done," Mona says. "I'm getting a perm next week. Plaits are for babies, don't you think?"

Yolanda already feels a thunk in her chest.

"Do you wear tampons?"

"No."

"You should. They don't show. All the girls at school wear them." Mona rakes her nails through her hair.

"Do you want to do each other's nails?"

"Not really."

Mona opens the door. "It's musty in here." She strips off like she's in the privacy of the bathroom.

First time Kee Kee passes the room, Mona's behind is up in the air as she steps out of her skirt and into the bottoms of her pajamas. When Joe Brown walks by, she is lying on her back in Yolanda's bed with her legs up in the air, looking like she's posing for a magazine, her hair spread out across a pillow, her arms arched out in a fake stretch so that her breasts lift up a little.

Yolanda is lying on the bed, trying to grab Mona's attention by moving on to the boy part of the conversation, but Mona is already distracted.

"Mona, do you really like Mouse? He looks nasty. Did you let him kiss you?"

"Uh huh."

"I like Junior, but he don't know. I wrote a note, but . . ."

Mona lets out a loud cackle like Miss Carter or Mama or Grandma Tookie, a laugh like that of the women at church. Not a girl's laugh, not even a teenage girl's laugh. A grown woman's laugh, as though a child has just said something cute. Yolanda grows sullen and tries to think of something that will help seal the crack, but she can't think of anything. She feels their friendship splitting open even wider in the quiet of the night.

Mona sits straddle-legged on Yolanda's bed. The second time Kee Kee walks by, Mona says she has to use the bathroom.

Moments later, Yolanda hears her brother say, "Get out of here girl," through the walls. But soon their voices are lowered, and she can hear the squeaking of the bedsprings and the muffled grunts. Then the moaning is so loud that Yolanda fears her father will awake and come to check things out. Later, she hears water running in the bathroom, but Mona still brings the smell of onions with her into the bedroom.

"Y'all out of toilet paper," Mona says.

Yolanda stares at her right between her nasty legs and rolls her eyes.

"What?" she says. "Didn't nothing happen."

The feeling of wanting to slap Mona rises up in Yolanda's chest again, but she can't do it. She can't move. All the fight in her has evaporated. She is tethered to the bed by the goings on of this night. She lies there and tries to find sleep, the nerves in her face twitching beneath her skin, her heart racing so fast she can hear it beating in her ears. *Flap, flap, flap.*

The Kitchen Ghosts.

The Goode Women
(Yolanda, Tookie, Minnie Mae)

It's snowing. Outside, Joe Brown breathes icy wind into his lungs, rubs his black gloves together, and scrapes the windows of the car. Inside the Goode house, the women make soup.

Minnie Mae rests in the living room chair, rising up every few minutes to make a suggestion. "Not too much," she says when Tookie sprinkles a second salting into the pot.

"Mama, I believe I know how to make soup." As Tookie quickly pulls the handle toward her, the heavy pot scrapes across the burner and makes an angry sound. She stirs the soup and bangs the spoon on the edge, shaking off the excess. Clearly fuming, she salts the pot again, then peppers it. Her brothers haven't visited since August, but over the last few months Tookie's anger has solidified in her guts. She can feel the residual of that July conversation clean up to her shoulders, which ache like a tooth now. And for the first time in her life, she cannot hold her tongue.

"Been making soup all my life."

"Don't look like you have. Don't look like you know nothing, putting all that salt in trying to kill us all. Get all our blood up."

Lucy is stirring cornbread batter and letting the skillet heat up in the oven.

Yolanda is lying in bed. There is no school today because of slick roads. Below her window, she hears the rumble of her father's truck, the loud scrape of the windshield ice, and Kee Kee's muffled voice blending with her father's. She hears the familiar bickering of the women. And while she lazes there, the covers pulled up around her chin, basking in her own warmth as though it was a womb cradle, she thinks of Mona and that nest they made together. Not the Mona who is her friend now. Not the Mona who even God thought was beautiful enough to deserve to rest on her birthday (that was why he made it snow, Yolanda is convinced). She is remembering the little girl Mona whom she loved more than anything. And more than dolls and tea sets, snowball fights and clubhouses, she misses Mona's hand in hers. She misses secrets. She misses huddling together by the heating vent on a winter day just like this one, a sheet spread across them rising up and blowing out like a balloon when the furnace fired on.

Later that evening, the snow melts enough that black spots show under the streetlights. Dirty footprints and huge piles of black snow appear where neighbors have shoveled their driveways and the exhaust pipes from their cars have dusted the mounds with soot. But the trees, even the ones on the hills that surround Opulence, still glisten with tufts of pure white snow and their icicle coats.

When Mona calls, Yolanda says her daddy will not let her go out on a school night—which it may not be since the snow is still on some of the back roads—though she doesn't even ask. So instead here she is alone, bored, tired of watching TV, tired of writing in her diary. She mopes and circles the house, moving from the kitchen, where she stops for a bowl of cereal, through Mama Minnie and Grandma Tookie's rooms, up the steps to her room, then back down again to the living room. She sits down, then gets back up to change the television, then cuts it off again.

Kee Kee is out. She isn't speaking to him either. He has stolen something from her, more than the last slice of cake or candy from her hidden stash or the last drop of orange juice this time. When he tried to talk to her, to poke her ribs in that big brother way, to muss up her hair, she weaved her body out of his grasp and left the room. She believes she could still smell Mona on the hand that he tried to grab her with.

Her parents have already gone to bed, though the sun has barely set. She listens at their door for a little while, long enough to hear her father say, "I love you, Lucy," and to hear her mother answer back with a loud sigh, then fast breathing like her parents have run somewhere fast and need water before they die. She has tried before to imagine her mother as a made-for-TV white woman, her head angled back in a romantic pose, and her father, rugged and handsome, wrinkling his brow with desire and pulling her close to him. But her parents are in their bedroom making their own kind of love, panting like dogs, grunting like pigs. Two old people. One smelling like car grease, the other one living in some world of her own creation. Yolanda shakes her head and moves on.

When she makes her third lap through the downstairs living room where Tookie and Minnie rest on the couch, she decides to plop herself on the bottom of the steps just to listen to them awhile. The stairs are behind their sitting place, so they don't know she's there. Yolanda, even at seventeen, sits with her eyes closed, playing a child's game of willing herself invisible. She has that way about her. There are even moments when she is fully present, but so quiet that no one remembers she had been in the room when some secret was discussed.

That is how she knows about Grandma Tookie's orange heart pills, how she knows about her father's stash of blackberry wine that nests in a sock in the basement, how she knows about her mother's trips to the head doctor.

"Lord God, that child's going to wear out the wood. Back and forth like a haint . . ."

"Her age is just coming on her. That's all."

"Hand me my balm, Tookie."

Yolanda doesn't hear her grandmother say anything but she knows she has followed her mother's orders when she smells the knee salve and hears Mama Minnie say thank you. When Yolanda peers around the wall, she can see Tookie, one knee on the floor, rubbing the liniment into Mama Minnie's joints. The two women are quiet, but exchange knowing looks.

She watches Tookie struggle back up to her knees and position herself on the couch. Mother and daughter sit side by side. It's on nights like this that any member of the family could pass by and see them sitting like this, staring off into space like they are trapped under amber together, a solid mass, frozen, remembering some day long ago. The three of them sit like this for a long time—the two elders on the couch and Yolanda hiding on the steps—until Tookie breaks the silence. This coiled and rusted thing in Tookie's chest finally frees itself, but it comes out crisp and clear, as if she has asked her mama for her sauerkraut recipe or said "Pass the pepper" or "Do you need something from the store?"

"Mama, why'd you beat me like that?"

Minnie Mae lets out a long sigh. "What's done is gone."

"I just want to know why, Mama. Many a girl around here . . ."

"Many a girl done been whipped by their mama, too."

"That wasn't no whipping."

Minnie Mae studies the air for a while, then says, "The boys done all moved off somewhere. You stayed here by your old mama. Maybe it did you some good."

"Why, Mama?" Tookie leans her head back into the sofa cushion and closes her eyes, waiting for an answer from Minnie Mae, from God, from somebody. Somebody needs to tell her something. So she can go on, move on past these minutes she is wallowing in.

"I expected more from you, I guess, Tookie. I don't rightly know." Minnie Mae tears up her face when a pain shoots through her hip, and hopes that Tookie will just shut up. Hopes seeing her mama in so much pain will be enough to make her hush.

Tookie pulls at the collar of her house dress, snaps the top two clasps and rubs up and down her own arms like she's cold.

"You cold? I can't stand this fool." Minnie Mae tries to pull Tookie into saying something about the man on television.

"Why, Mama?"

In all these years, she has never asked. But something in the night has grabbed ahold of Tookie's throat and opened it up wide and long enough to set words free. Minnie Mae pats her own knees like a song is playing somewhere.

"Why?" Tookie says again, her voice rising up louder and louder each time.

"I wasn't having no whores in my house, Tookie."

"But I wasn't . . ."

"You should have kept your legs closed. Period. Maybe it didn't do you no good. Seems like you still ain't got a bit of sense."

And Tookie begins to cry. She cries so long and so hard that she can't see her mother struggle to rise from the couch and go to her bedroom. She can feel the weight easing from that side of the couch, but she can't see a thing. There's a piece of gauze around the whole world.

The night Lucy was born, June found Tookie in the bathroom, standing in her own water, and ran to get their mother.

Mama was like a wild woman, not allowing an ambulance, not allowing Daddy to take her to the hospital. Leaving her there on the bathroom floor in a heap of suffering for nearly nine hours before the baby came, then Minnie Mae tying the cord and cleaning up the baby herself and putting her in Tookie's thirteen-year-old arms. It was only then that her mother touched her forehead and pushed back her hair. And it was in those few seconds of touch that Tookie swam. She recalled how good her mother's fingers had felt on her head. And long after Minnie Mae had left the room that night and left her alone to her new mothering duties, Tookie basked in the solace of her mother's hand.

She remembers it even now as the one good thing that would carry her over.

When Tookie rises from the couch to make her way down the hallway to her room for the night, Yolanda watches her walk, studies the droop in her shoulders, sees a bit of one of the scars rising above the neckline of her housedress. Although she still doesn't entirely know what the conversation was about, she knows she has borne witness to something old, something still not over.

When she hears the click of Tookie's door, Yolanda lies on the couch where the women have been. The warmth of Tookie's body is still there on the cushions, and Yolanda falls off to sleep.

She dreams of a wedding—a glorious wedding with morning glories and sunflowers from the old homeplace, and honeysuckle vine, bright red hummingbirds, and a great long yellow dress with a high collar and shiny buttons, and the bride's face covered by a veil as long as the dress. Through the mesh Yolanda sees a woman's face, but she isn't sure if it is her own. She doesn't feel like a bride in the dream; more like somebody watching, not from the audience, but with a bird-like view, watching the woman in the gown ready herself. And just as day breaks and the bride is about to reveal her face, Lucy comes down the steps humming and pulls Yolanda from her sleep.

"Yolanda, get to bed before you catch a crick in your neck."

In her bed, with the covers over her head, Yolanda tries to recapture the bride, the veil almost lifted, but the dream is gone, flown itself out of her head. Her mind follows the worn path back to the beginning, and she's only a little surprised that at this moment she can only think in small disconnected spurts, like an old movie reel spinning: a blue sweater, the smell of pine, a large bird's nest.

1979

The Crow in the House.

Tookie

Birds were always a sure sign.

She sees the crow, perched high up on the what-not shelf, sitting between a glass replica of the Statue of Liberty and a tiny ceramic boy walking a yellow dog.

The bird pecks at the head of the boy.

She ignores it for a time, then watches it fly around the living room, lighting on the lamp, at the top of the curtains, on the fireplace. She watches it fly against the closed window, then back to the lampshade. She hears the bird rustle its feathers. As she looks out the window, a branch cracks, falls from high up in the oak tree.

As usual, when she is alone, she walks back and forth across the living room floor, hands clutched in front of her, both remembering and trying not to.

She has a headache.

She is sleepy, but refuses to lie down and nap. She keeps her eyes on the yard, looking from tree to tree, flower to flower, but her thoughts are beyond this time and place.

It's 1943. She is scared. She is as surprised to know that she is carrying a baby as she was when Bruce Harrison took her to the center of the cornfield and kissed her so hard she thought she would die. He took her clothes off, promised it wouldn't hurt. Promised he'd take it out before anything bad happened. But when he climbed on top of her it had hurt like nothing she had ever known, and then he had mounted her and put all his weight into her chest and pushed inside her and began to move faster and faster, like he was trying to kill something, and wouldn't stop. She knew it was wrong then. Knew it was the "anything bad" that he had talked about that was happening. Tried to close herself up down there, to close the space that she had opened up. And when she ran home and found blood stains in her panties, even though she knew it wasn't her time of the month, she wanted to go tell her mother right there and then, but she didn't. So she just prayed and prayed that nothing else bad would happen, but then it did. Minnie hadn't told her about babies, but Tookie knew she was pregnant the way any woman knows. Her menses stopped, breasts grew swollen, sickness came. Baby in there. And who else would a child turn to but her mama—the one who had been there to nurse her cuts and bruises, the one who had stayed up with her for three days when she had the fever and changed the ice rags on her head and sung her songs. Who else but a mama would understand this?

But Tookie had barely got the words from her mouth before Minnie Mae said, "I didn't raise you to be no whore!" Then the strap of the belt.

"Mama, I didn't know."

"Knew enough to spread your legs. Knew that didn't you?"

Each word came with a lash on her back. With her back turned to protect the baby, she couldn't see her mother's face, but she could hear her labored breathing. Heard the shuffle of footsteps behind her when her daddy tried to pull the belt from her mama's hands. Could see her brothers cowering in the corners of the kitchen and see their scared faces begging their mother to stop.

She remembers her father finally pulling her mother away, her brothers slinking off grateful that the beating had finally stopped. Remembers being in a house full with two adults and two children and having nobody to comfort her. Remembers pulling her own bruised and bloodied body up and going to the bathroom, taking a bath and crawling, sore and marked for life, into the bed. Remembers wishing for her mother's touch on her forehead, on her arm, somewhere. Remembers needing her mother's healing hand.

Tookie taps her head, trying to settle back into the present, gazes out into the yard until she hears the car pull up and the voices of Minnie Mae, Lucy, and the baby girl coming into the house. She rubs her arms. The crow flies back above her head and lands on the curtain rod above the window where she stands. Tookie looks at the crow, sees its jet-black eyes on her. Looks straight ahead, takes in the warmth of the sun.

"Well, now you've done your job," she says. "I ain't mad. How could I be?"

The crow has been in the house for an hour before Tookie scoots it out the open window with a broom, just as the others are coming back into the house.

1980

Spooning Tomatoes.
Long Night.
Accustomed to Death.

Mona

The daffodils are blooming, and women all over Opulence are spring-cleaning. Mona is helping Francine hang the bedclothes on the line. The setting sun gives Opulence an orange hue in the evening. The April breeze whips at Mona's skirt. Her mother is working her to death—washing down walls, airing the linen, polishing the windows. After supper will come a long night of spooning hot tomatoes into plastic containers for the deep freezer, to be squeezed in next to all the rest, and then the making of ice cream.

Since Yolanda has deserted her, the house is too quiet. Mona grows bored with Francine. She spends her time in her room, staring up at flowered patterns on the wallpaper or the cracks in the ceiling, daydreaming herself a future, which mostly includes being in some man's arms. She listens to music on her portable eight-track player, bored to pieces the majority of the time, although she manages to sneak out once or twice a week.

Mona has taken up with Marshall Ross, a married factory worker who lives in Lancaster. Marshall has children almost her age. When she met him in the aisle of the dime store, she was trying to decide whether to buy lip gloss or a set of jacks with her allowance. She knew that the time for jacks had passed, but the bright blue metal ones and their bright red ball stopped her cold before Marshall turned the corner and said, "You are one fine woman." Being only seventeen, hearing this man—who wasn't half bad looking—refer to her as a woman turned something inside her.

He must be Mr. Brown's age, was the first thing that came into her mind before she said, "Well, you a good-looking man. I always did love me a caramel brother." And she licked her lips, curling her tongue up high near her nostrils, then easing it slowly back into her mouth like that kind of woman.

Marshall seemed a little startled at first, because he knew full well that this was not in fact a woman, but when she walked closer to him with a certain saunter in her hipbones, his breath left him completely.

"Sure would be nice to have . . ." Mona slowed down a little for show, " . . . a cold bottle of pop."

Marshall nearly ran to the cooler at the front counter to buy her a Grape Nehi.

Mona is pleased with herself: a real man, with a real car, a real job. She has spent months now making up excuses to Francine, brainstorming with Marshall to try and come up with reasons to get out of the house.

The first time she went out with him, they met down by the creek. She told Francine she needed a walk, that her feelings had been so hurt by Yolanda's rejection. Of course it was true, she hadn't talked to Yolanda in months, but she ran down the hill at the allotted time to meet Marshall, then corrected herself when she felt childish, and walked her mother's straight-backed walk the remainder of the way.

It was there, in the front seat of Marshall's car, where she experienced her first set of man's hands, not the bumbling, groping-fingered touch of boys her age or the hurried fingers of Kee Kee, but the confident stroke of a grown man.

Mona almost smirks as she follows the orders that Francine whispers out like somebody's school teacher.

"Mona, grab that basket, will you?"

"Mona, don't fold the sheets that way."

"Mona, honey, why don't you do the living room windows over, they're smeared."

And she completes all of her chores with a smile, not only because Francine's loudness is never loud at all, but because she knows her reward is coming, if not this evening, then the next or the next.

She hates it when Marshall doesn't show up at their agreed meeting spot, but grown-ass men have things to do. He told her so, and she had seen it herself—watching Joe Brown's heavy hands always repairing something. Grown men have things to do. Sometimes she tries to imagine Marshall at home with his wife and children—eating dinner or laughing at the television. But mostly she envisions herself doing those things with him, and the times they would have afterward in the bedroom, with no mothers and no wives to interfere.

She is thinking of one of those times right after supper, while she and Francine are spooning the lukewarm liquid of the scalded tomatoes into the three-quart containers, when the phone rings. It startles them both.

Mona picks up the phone, halfway hoping that it's Marshall saying, "I'm tired of hiding. I love you. Tell your mother I'm coming to get you," but it isn't him.

Yolanda's voice is weak and sweet. Mona cradles the receiver and sits silent, listening, hoping to hear the hollers and belly laughs that are usually present in the background at the Goode house, but she hears nothing but silence.

"Who is it, Mona?" Francine comes from the kitchen into the living room, drying her hands on her apron, a large questioning V in the center of her forehead. *Ugly*, Mona is thinking to herself, *My mother is ugly.*

"It's Yolanda. Her Grandmamma Tookie died." She cups the phone, protecting Yolanda from hearing that word *died*.

"Did she suffer?" The words seem thick and useless on Mona's tongue as soon as she offers them, but all the children of Opulence have become accustomed to death and the words that get flung out. *Did she suffer?*

She hears Yolanda take a sigh as though she were gathering breath for the next words: "No, no she didn't suffer," Yolanda says. "She was right peaceful," and she sounds old too. They both do. They sound like their mothers.

Blest Be the Tie That Binds.

At the funeral, Mona makes her way through the crowd and sits beside Yolanda in one of the family pews. She glances over her shoulder at her mother, who looks solemn and alone in the back of the church. Then she notices how most of the parishioners are paired up. Even the tiniest of children's heads bob in twos. She glances back at Francine again, feels a bit of concern for her mother there all alone, but knows that Yolanda needs her more.

The girls sit side by side in silence throughout the service, their spreading hips straining the loose material of their Sunday dresses. Mona wants to tell Yolanda she likes her hair this way, swirled to one side and flipped under like a movie star. And Yolanda wants to tell Mona that her burgundy-tinted lip gloss is perfect for her complexion, not too bright or gaudy. But instead they manage closed-lip glances at each other from time to time. And when Lucy cries out, "Mama, please don't leave me," in the middle of the service, Mona puts her arm around Yolanda and lets her weep into her shoulder.

Reverend Townsend preaches a good sermon, makes it sound like Tookie was the purest, most saintly woman in the church, which makes some of the old women squirm in the pews, clear their throats, and glance at one another over reading glasses, because they remember a fast-tailed Tookie who brought all that shame on her mama's name.

The Senior Choir, dressed in the new red-and-white robes that Minnie Mae bought for them, belts out "Blest Be the Tie That Binds" with their quivering voices, swaying back and forth, some with their eyes closed, some with their hands waving like branches in the wind, trying to send Tookie to glory in style. Occasionally, one of the women in the audience gets happy and shouts, throwing her body up and back over the pew, and is quickly rescued by some fan-wielding usher wearing white gloves. The deacons shout "Amen!" even some of the ones who were guilty of sniffing after Tookie's skirt tail in her young days. Even the parishioners who are not grieving so much for Tookie, but recalling the funerals of their own mothers, their own sisters, their own wives, sing the songs as loud as they can, and pray hard for Tookie's soul.

Back in the corner of the church, on the back row some distance from Francine, is a man that everyone thinks they know. A man who has lived in Opulence forever, and is of course somebody's child, somebody's husband, somebody's something. He's the type of man who is handsome enough alright, but quiet and invisible. Doesn't talk too much and often goes unnoticed. He is aging, yet handsome still, whiteness dancing a regal pattern through his black curly hair. He looks on. With Tookie's death, a secret is lost, and he is the only other person in the world who knows it. Tookie's death isn't something that he is happy about; that would make him cruel and heartless, and he isn't.

It was so many years ago, and he strains to see a young Tookie up under him in a field, her narrow body writhing beneath his own. He remembers it tenderly, not like the lecherous memory of an old man. It bothers him to see Lucy grieving for her mother and him unable to offer comfort. Lucy has the same brown eyes and hollow ridge along her cheekbone as his other girls. She is more beautiful, in fact, than some of the others, but he can't tell her so, not now, after all these years.

He allows himself to remember the trust in Tookie's eyes that day when he took her in the cornfield. He hadn't loved her, but she hadn't been what some of them say she was. He knows she loved him as much as a thirteen-year-old could. And now, as an old man, when he thinks of that evening and its pureness, he feels tears well up in his eyes. He glances over at the Clark woman and takes up his cane and leaves before anyone's suspicions begin to grow.

Minnie Mae sits on the front row, peering toward the casket where Tookie's body is on display. Tears travel the creases, then fall off her face. She carries a new sadness, the likes of which nobody in the Goode family has ever seen her have. Kee Kee tries to comfort his great-grandmother, goes over to give Minnie Mae a hug or a hand to hold—anything he can do—but when he reaches her she raises up her arthritic right hand and shakes her head, no, and shoos him away.

Butter and June and their families sit side by side along their own pew. They pat each other's shoulders in comfort and then go up and sit with their mother for a while, but they slip out before dinner after the funeral and head on back to the city. Later, they will talk on the phone, solidifying plans to sell the homeplace. "It's time," Butter will say. June will agree, but will look out the window at his manicured yard and cry.

At the interment, Lucy looks up between her tears and for a flash of a moment notices Yolanda and Mona, their backs turned to her, side by side. Yolanda's head leans over toward Mona's shoulder, their torsos comfortable against one another like two women friends united.

Joe Brown places his arm around Lucy's waist. They

take in deep breaths as they make their way across the cemetery. They lean against one another and watch Yolanda, her back turned to them, becoming a woman before their very eyes. Joe Brown feels like years are somehow missing, like he has just figured something out, too late to do anything about it. Above their heads, they hear the clamoring of birds and then their singing. Joe Brown thinks they are there to check on Tookie, to cheer her on into glory.

Need Is a Four-Letter Word.

Mona

Mona Clark holds her bus ticket in one hand and in the other a suitcase filled with her clothes. She balances her pocketbook on her thin shoulder and gets in line. She doesn't know how long she will be able to wear the hip-huggers or the tight-knit blouses. She pats her navel, as if she has simply eaten too much. Once she reaches the city she will find work.

She tries to picture herself settled into a city apartment, lying in her new bed at night, listening to the steady buzz of cars from the highway; steady work at a clothing store perhaps, where she will say, "May I help you?" and the customers will say how beautiful she is. Like a model, they will say. And she even sees herself with a new man. He will be stout and strong-jawed, drive a nice car, and call her "Sugar." And his eyes, she can see his eyes already, brown and sparkly wet like periwinkles, and always on her. But she hasn't really thought about the baby. It's not even a baby yet. She closes her eyes and tries to imagine what a child of hers might look like. A girl, no, a boy, who might favor the daddy she has never known. Maybe a girl, though women in general can't be trusted. A son is what she needs, although *need* is a four-letter word, large as the world.

Mona squeezes her eyes together against the sun and the

tears and is startled by what she sees, the red behind her eye-lids. The red, just like Yolanda said when they were girls. She laughs aloud until she notices a woman at the front of the line turning to stare at her.

She wants to remember all the parts of Opulence she sees. To her right, the gentle outline of the houses on Depot Street. To her left, the road that leads to Carter's Grocery and the hills beyond, the morning's mist rising above them like smoke in a rich man's pipe.

She watches the black loop of the street until it ribbons down another hill and disappears from her view. She breathes deep and takes in the spicy pine, the soil, the morning dew, the rising sun. If she breathes deep enough she thinks she can smell the pecan swirls behind the counter at Carter's; Miss Lucy's gingerbread; her mother's cornbread cooling on the stove. She tries to condense all of Opulence into something small and attractive that she can fold up and carry with her—Hickory Grove hill in the summertime; Yolanda's smile; Dinner on the Grounds; all the days of high school; the smell of oil and gas where Joe Brown works on cars.

The bus pulls into the gas station, big and shiny silver, windows tinted dark green, the smell of diesel. The driver steps off, grabs Mona's bag, and deposits it into the underbelly of the bus before she has time to think or breathe or change her mind. And she was almost there, right on the edge of changing her mind, but his quick actions propel her along. With a deep sigh she climbs aboard with the driver holding her elbow. He is a white man, red and puffy, round like a dumpling, but even he can't ignore the silhouette of her long, dark legs sprouting beneath the miniskirt.

Once aboard, she looks for friendly faces, but Mona has not turned out to be the kind of woman whom other women smile at. She is met with eye rolls and slant-eyed stares. The wives loop arms with their husbands as Mona presses by them, as if by simply touching them she could claim pieces of them for herself. Some of the men lean slightly into the aisle, just so they can touch Mona in some small way, with their shoulders, their elbows, their eyes. She makes her way toward the back of the bus, trying to look as sophisticated as possible, not country at all if she can help it. She even stops to straighten her skirt and pull down her blouse.

But as much as she has longed for this, this freedom to do what she pleases, now that it has come, she isn't sure. It has only been six weeks since she and Yolanda graduated from high school, and now here she is.

Already things are so different. Yolanda, she imagines, will be just like the other women in Opulence: devoted to her husband, children galore, Sunday school and PTA meetings, and forever somebody's somebody telling her something about somebody else. She imagines Yolanda fat with long dresses and a hump in her back like her mother's. Junior grunting and snorting, hollering, "Woman where's supper?!" She's sure of it. Can see it coming. Mona has grown so tired of this place where everyone knows your kin—even the best parts of it.

"Ain't you Francine's girl?"

"Yes." And always they pretend that it's good news.

"Well I know your mama's all proud of you grown up into such a pretty thing."

And for a moment she regrets any additional shame that she may have brought on her mother's head. She tries to shake her mother's crying from her ears. Shame can't last always. Can it? Everyone in Opulence knows her, and she is glad to be going somewhere where no one does.

Yolanda's wedding was small. No wedding dress or tuxedo or bridesmaids. It was sticky hot, so they held the wedding on the grounds. Yolanda was pretty, wearing a simple flowered dress with baby's breath and lavender in her Afro. And Mr. Brown and Kee Kee in suits and ties was a sight to see. They stood awkward and beautiful through the ceremony. Junior was handsome in some plain sort of way. A big Afro and a goofy smile a mile wide between narrow lips. As they all stood there, Mona in the position of maid of honor, she couldn't help remembering what she'd done with Kee Kee, and kissing Junior one time when they were in middle school.

They'd been at the skating rink and she stopped just short of running into him, and kissed him, open-mouthed and long. She couldn't say why she had done it. She just had, and she had enjoyed seeing him flustered and guilty for not pushing her away sooner.

She hesitates at the thought for a minute. Her jaw tightens against any pain she has caused. Nothing has turned out as she intended.

Marshall had promised to leave his wife. She had waited to be brought out of the shadows and into the broad light of day.

Once, at the highlight of their romance, he took her to The Knights Inn. There he held her like a wife, long, without rush or worry. They sat cross-legged in the bed naked and ate potato chips and Nabs from the vending machine. When they grew thirsty, they intertwined one another's arms and drank cans of grape pop like it was champagne.

"You are truly my pretty girl," Marshall whispered in her ear, his breath smelling of cigarettes and pop, and Mona rubbed the rise in his belly and held her arm there and squeezed.

"I love you."

Apart from lifting her skirt in the shadows of a parking lot, or the wet heat of his breath in her ear in the cramped backseat of his car, Mona felt loved.

Mona is good at solving puzzles. All her life, she has been deciphering one thing or another. So when she put her mind to it, it wasn't hard to remember Marshall's phone number when she saw it on a bill in the floorboard of the car one night. After that, it wasn't long before she had retrieved his address from the glove box while he stepped into the bushes to pee. But it took her a long time to use them. She just gathered information and placed it in a small candle box: the receipt from the motel, a button from his shirt, a blue carnation that he had given her on her birthday, his phone number and his address, all the letters that she had written to him tied in a ribbon. She never thought of it as evidence. Just things she would keep to show to their children.

But then Marshall began to lie. "Can't come tonight, I've got to work overtime." "One of the kid's is sick." "She going somewhere and I got to keep the kids." Mona wanted proof.

The first time she drove her mother's car by the house, she drove quickly, afraid that he might see her. But eventually she knew the turn of Marshall's street as well as she knew her own. She knew the woman with the wild red hair lived three houses down. That the gray house with blue shutters was abandoned. That the people in 729 had a mean dog. And she knew what time they turned lights on after supper and when the lights were turned off before bed.

She sat across the street some nights, watching them like she would a movie. Marshall coming through the door at five thirty on a night when he had told her he had to work late. The wife, whom Mona had imagined as homely and wrinkled, but who was in fact attractive, with a young smiling face. She greeted him at the door with a hug or a kiss. The children nestled around them like mice. She watched him bring in groceries and mow the yard. But none of it made her angry; she knew she had to be patient. Sometimes she didn't see his car pull in at all, which meant he had told her the truth. It made her smile.

She had never intended on using the phone number. It was just a piece of him that she enjoyed fondling. But as her meetings with Marshall grew infrequent, she progressed from dialing it all the way through and hanging up before it rang to allowing someone to pick it up. When the wife answered, Mona hung up. When the children answered, she listened to their voices and imagined her own children having the same glee.

"Mama, ain't nobody saying nothing," they would say, and she would hang up.

When Marshall answered, her heart soared. She closed her eyes and listened to his voice. Even as he grew angry, she listened.

"Hello . . . Hello . . . Hello. Who in the hell is this?"

And she went to bed satisfied, even if she didn't get to see him.

For sixty days she tried to will blood into her panties, prayed, even delighted at the cramps she thought she felt. For sixty days.

One night when he met her in the park, after a long pause and downcast eyes, Mona straightened her back and said, "I'm pregnant." She said it matter-of-fact, as if she were saying, "Oh Marshall look. I have broken a fingernail."

The night before, while she lay in bed, she had imagined Marshall taking her into his arms and telling her that they would keep the baby and start a family. Everything would be fine.

"It ain't mine."

Mona said nothing.

"I'm married, girl. You knew that."

There was so much she wanted to say. She wanted to suddenly become one of the women she'd seen up on Maxwell who would spar with a man. She had seen it hundreds of times on sleepy summer nights when she and Yolanda were somewhere in grown folks' business. They had been there when Venus Carter slapped her man cold in the street, bloodied his nose and laid him out like she was Muhammad Ali. They had seen Bessie Paradise scratch all the hide off Boney Williams, leaving long red lightning streaks across his yellow face. They saw the pretty, big-boned Etta Bates stab toward husband Frankie with all her might until her long good hair shook down out of its bun and covered her face and shoulders like a shroud. She tried to summon the fire of all those women she'd known all her life.

But she couldn't speak, couldn't conjure any of those voices in her head. *Motherfucker, what you mean? You sorry black bastard. I'd just as soon see you dead.* All those women were speaking in her ears, but her own words failed her. She stood in silence and cried.

"You been good to me, pretty girl," he said. Marshall drew her close to him, an action she mistook for a change of heart, and kissed her long and slow. His hands moved from the small of her back to the roundness of her behind and then to the tenderness of her upright breasts. He cupped them like apples and moved his hand up her dress tail and down between her legs. He struggled with her panties and allowed his fingers to slide into there. Mona leaned toward him.

It's going to be alright, she thought.

It wasn't a cruel thing, really, she would think later.

"I'm going to miss this," he said, and released her. The elastic waist of her panties snapped like a rubber band and she could feel the sting of a welt forming where it landed on her waist. Marshall walked away.

She could see herself clawing on his back like a wildcat. *Naw, motherfucker. Motherfucker, what you mean?* But words solidified in her throat, taking her breath with them. Marshall never even turned around. The night was suddenly cold and black; the stars had fallen so low she thought she could reach out and catch them.

Marshall started his Cadillac and was gone.

The night before she left, she called to hear his voice again. With her mother yelling on her end, and the children yelping and running in the background on Marshall's, she could barely hear his voice, but she cradled the phone as if it were his face in her hands.

"Hello . . . Hello . . ."

"I love you."

The first time, she just mouthed it into the phone.

"Hello . . . Hello . . ."

"I love you."

This second time, a whisper just loud enough to break through Francine's tirade.

"Girl, who are you talking to on that telephone?"

It was someone else's voice in her mother's mouth.

"Who is this?"

"You tell that sorry-ass boy he's got responsibilities. You better be telling him that . . ."

Francine, who was usually quiet and somber as a cow, was pacing around Mona like a caged cat, around and around in a half circle.

"I love you."

This time, Mona's words were louder, a pleading lilt in her voice.

"I love you."

"Love him? You tell that bastard . . ."

Francine was someone else, a crazy woman.

"Bitch, don't call this house anymore."

Click and then a heartbreaking dial tone.

Mona felt like a mourner at a funeral. A woman whose man had died. A woman like her mother.

On the bus, Mona fidgets with her skirt. She goes through her pocketbook, reading business cards and the backs of packs of matches and old doctor bills and her report cards. She thinks of Yolanda, who has always had Joe Brown and Kee Kee and now Junior. She thinks of her mother only once, and then watches the couple in front of her, the woman nesting her long, skinny face into the man's shoulder.

1994

Girls Everywhere.

Kee Kee

His wife, Nadine, refuses to call him Kee Kee. Sounds like a girl's name to her. It's one of those nicknames that stuck as soon as he was born. He thought it was no different than Butterball or Fat Baby or Slim or June Bug. He's heard these names all his life. Her family is not the type to do such a thing. Her people are always dressed like church, even on Friday nights and lazy Sunday afternoons. They are black cardboard cutouts: perfect house, perfect children (one girl, one boy), and a Chihuahua named Perro.

Nadine saunters into the room naked, like she's on a model's runway, her hair swooped up into a curly ponytail, the new version of the Afro puff. Kee Kee pulls her close and rubs her belly. She puts her hands on her hips and stands to the side.

"Showing?" she says.

He loves her when she's playful like this. "Look at you, Little Mama," he says.

Nadine falls into Kee Kee's arms and kisses him. He can feel his calloused fingers against her soft back.

"Five months?" he says.

She nods, kisses both of his cheeks before she stands up and slips on her robe.

Before they were married, when someone would ask him if he had any children, he would say, "Not that I know of." It was an old joke, and everybody laughed, but it was true. He didn't know for sure. At night when he was lying in bed, the possibility of a child somewhere was always in the back of his mind. Kee Kee imagined a little girl with barrettes on her plaits, two proud front teeth.

He has opened his mouth many times to tell Nadine about the possibility, but the words won't come out. "Kevin?" she calls out to him when he stares out into the space between them. At these times, he is conjuring this daughter of his. He sees her jumping around in circles or running through the house. She is light-skinned, a pretty little thing, just like Ina.

Nadine sits at the kitchen table, crosses her legs, and spins her wedding and engagement rings around her finger. As Kevin scrambles eggs, stirs fried apples, and butters toast, he realizes that he's as good in the kitchen as any woman in his family. He can kitchen dance like any Goode woman with a skillet. And can also do a mean dance with the inside of a car's engine, just like his daddy.

These days, he makes a modest living amongst the grease and grime of his own garage. Doesn't pay much, but the steady stream of townspeople keeps Nadine in clothes and keeps the light bill and the house note paid.

After breakfast, Kevin slips into his green coveralls with the wide patch that reads *Brown's Garage*. Nadine pulls on a black suit for her job as a teller down at the bank; the skirt strains across her belly.

"Maternity clothes are so damn ugly," she says. "I'm trying to stay away from them." She turns back and forth in front of the mirror, rubbing a smooth straight line across the horizon of her belly.

Kevin is quiet.

He and Nadine met at a bookstore. Though he didn't consider himself the smartest cat, he read every now and then. A customer in the garage had told him he should read Richard Wright, so he went in to order *Black Boy*. He already had a small, neat shelf over his bed filled with James Baldwin, Langston Hughes, LeRoi Jones, and Samuel Delany. He even had a little Stephen King and George Orwell. When he saw Nadine, he knew she was not the type of sister who would give out her phone number easily. But six months later they were negotiating one another's kitchens and bathrooms as though they had been together their entire lives.

When he kisses Nadine goodbye, she turns her head, warning him not to mess up her lipstick. He thinks of this as he starts the truck up and backs out of the driveway. Nadine is the type of woman who puts a towel down before sex, and strips off the bed afterwards. She nags him if his boxers are on the bathroom floor too long. Their children, he thinks, will sparkle like his mother-in-law's silver.

In his rearview mirror, Kevin realizes that he has neglected to pick out his hair. It surprises him that Nadine said nothing about this. He leaves his hair uncombed, his small fro pressed to one side, in protest.

He has always needed a woman's attention, though the attention from the women in his family seemed to stop when his sister was born. He went from the wonderful and glorious Kee Kee Brown to big brother Kevin, carrier of diapers, peeler of potatoes, assistant to his father as he fixed things.

Years before he married Nadine, Kevin looked at other men with their children and wondered what kind of father he would have been. He wondered if he and Ina would have gotten along.

He thinks of Nadine's little cousin, Amie. A bright-eyed girl about the age his daughter would be, if she existed. The little round-faced girl tried to snuggle up against Nadine at the wedding. Nadine said, "Amie, don't get my dress dirty." She hugged the child at arm's length. The girl looked at him shyly before she removed her finger from her mouth, waved at him, and ran back to her mother.

Maybe his ghost girl was jealous: she came to him at that moment and refused to leave all during the reception, and even later up into the evening.

He watched Nadine that night and couldn't picture her as anyone's mama. He knew she would become the mother of his children, but he couldn't imagine her with a large stomach or a waddling ass back then. He couldn't see her cleaning up baby vomit or shit. He shook his head at the thought of her in one of those nice suits, changing a dirty diaper.

On his wedding night, while he slept with Nadine in the crook of his arm, he dreamt of his child. The girl appeared in a yellow dress in every wedding photograph. He didn't know how he would explain her image there.

"Who's this?" Nadine would ask.

"My baby girl," he would answer.

Nadine stirred in her sleep as though she was experiencing some kind of nightmare, her pressed hair plastered to one side of her face.

Kevin works on old man Kak Simpson's engine. He and Bug, the high school ace who works for him now, hoist the engine up with a pulley supported by several feet of heavy chain. Now that his hands are black and greasy, he'll let Bug and the engine crew take over. It isn't something he has to do anymore, but Kevin likes getting his hands sullied. Nothing like hard work. He got that much from his daddy. Joe Brown is a working man. Hands always moving across something.

Monique, who works up front in the office, calls Kevin on the loudspeaker. He sees the third line of the phone flashing red and knows Nadine's on the line. He hesitates.

"Kee Kee, line three!"

Though he can't see her, he knows that Monique has her thick fist on her hip, rolling her eyes toward the wall.

"Kevin," Nadine says, "how's your day?"

"Same old stuff."

"Mama and Daddy want to come by for dinner."

"I'll be working 'til seven."

"You're the boss. You can do whatever you want."

Kevin shifts his weight from his left leg to his right, wipes black grease on the thighs of his coveralls, picks some from his fingernails.

"Baby, let me call you back."

Ina was fine; a college sophomore from Indianapolis. He met her in the mall. He's met so many sisters while he was out shopping. This thought makes him smile now. He was coming out of the record store when he found Ina thumbing through the new albums.

"If you want it, it's yours," he said, when he saw her flipping over a classic Rick James. "It's yours, baby," he said again as he stepped toward her, his voice an octave below his normal voice. Cool-as-ice. He winked.

Ina laughed. "So you Barry White now?" she said. "That all you got?"

Kevin met Ina's parents once when they came down to visit. Her daddy reminded him of that Thurston cat on *Gilligan's Island*; his back was so straight Kevin thought he'd break if the wind blew the right way. The mother had an air like that too, her nose up toward the ceiling like she was always smelling shit. *Maybe I'm just drawn to these kinda fake-ass people*, he thinks now.

They were the same age, but sometimes Ina went over his head when she began talking her college talk. He could have gone to college too with his good grades, but he didn't. When he didn't have a clue what she was talking about, he just said "dig, dig," like he understood.

Ina called him late one night, her voice quivering like something was hung in her throat.

"You're what?"

His head was fogged. He wanted to say, "It ain't mine," like he'd seen brothers do, but he knew it most likely was his. They listened to each other's breathing through the receivers until Ina said, "Kee Kee, you hear me? You still there?"

"Uh huh."

"They want me to go away to have it and put it up for adoption."

"What? That sounds like some bougie . . . Wait a minute, Ina. I'll help you. I'll be a man."

"Mama and Daddy said no, Kee Kee."

"Ina you twenty years old . . ."

"I've got to finish school." She started crying.

"Do you think we should get an abortion?"

That felt bad as soon as it came out of his mouth.

"*We?* Kee Kee, there ain't no *we*."

Phone went dead.

When he tried to call back, all he got was a busy signal. When he finally got through a week later, Ina's roommate answered the phone.

"She gone."

"Gone? What do you mean she's gone."

"G-O-N-E. Packed up. Moved out."

"She leave a phone number?"

"Nope."

If Kevin said he'd tried hard to find her he'd be lying.

At the rehearsal dinner, he looked down the long table and scared even himself when he realized how many of the women he had been with. It was bragging rights to some of the cats he hung with, but it made him uncomfortable. He thought about what Mama Minnie or Granny Tookie would say. Disrespecting women. At least that's how they'd see it. That much he knew for sure.

Trudy, his brother-in-law Junior's sister, was the first girl he'd ever had.

Mona was still the one he was most ashamed of. It wasn't rape, but he knew she'd been too damned young. He had wanted to apologize to her for years, but never had the opportunity. She still looked him straight in the eye though, stared until he looked away.

Athena, who worked for the catering service, winked at him as she spooned gravy over roast beef on each dinner guest's plate. He looked around to make sure nobody noticed.

After the rehearsal dinner, back at his apartment, Ray-Ray and Kenny knocked on the door at nine. Even though he'd always thought that his aces would be the type of brothers who would have bachelor parties with hookers and strippers, his party was a drinking-walk-down-memory-lane-remember-when type of affair.

By ten o'clock, they were all drunk. Their laughter came in waves across his one-bedroom apartment. Boisterous laughter crashed through, then rippled down to silence, before somebody else brought up some other crazy thing they'd done as boys.

Late into the night, when they were full of liquor and stories and had begun a friendly game of spades, the telephone rang. Hearing his sister's voice on the phone always took him back to childhood.

"Hey, Pudge," he said.

"Yolanda," she said, correcting him, but he immediately heard some kind of misery in her voice.

"What's wrong, Pudge?"

"Just calling. My big brother's jumping the broom, ain't he?"

"Right."

"I hope she knows that she is marrying the most hard-headed . . ."

"Corny."

Yolanda laughed, but sounded like she had a cold. Like she'd been crying.

"You sick, Pudge?"

"No."

"Junior messing around on you again?"

"Not that I know of."

"You think he is?"

"Not sure."

"You got the blues . . . again?"

There was no answer.

"You been sick, Pudge?"

"Hope not."

He could almost feel her heart pounding. Just like Mama.

"You talked to Mama?" he said.

"No."

He held the phone until her breathing slowed, and knew that before he went to bed he would have to call his father.

"Pudge, try and get some sleep. Junior there?"

"Yes, he is, Kee Kee."

He hated it when she answered him like a little girl's foot stomp and crossed arms came with it. He heard Junior and his niece Shawna in the background.

"Tell Shawna I love her. Tell Junior he better take care of you. I love you, Pudge."

The brothers in the room laughed.

"Tell them to kiss it," Yolanda said before she hung up the phone.

It was well past midnight when all of his friends stumbled out, leaving Kevin's apartment filled with half-empty beer cans and bottles of liquor, potato chips growing stale in the heat. They had been too loud, and it took a moment for Kevin to adjust to the sudden quiet when he shut the door behind them, but then he remembered that these were his last few hours alone.

Joe answered on the first ring.

"Daddy? You still up?"

"We both are."

Before Kevin had a chance to apologize, his father asked about the wedding, sounding as though he was really too busy, but had a duty to ask.

"Wedding's fine. Too late to run off now."

His father laughed. "I guess so," he said.

"I'm calling about Pudge. Seems like she's not doing too well."

"Neither is your mama."

Before he hung up, he heard his mother in the background saying, "It's all gonna work itself out."

Alone in the dark, he thought of Nadine. He tried to imagine telling her about all of his past girlfriends, and her cocking her head in disbelief. He thought of telling her about his child, and the two of them agreeing to search the ends of the earth together until they found her. He thought of how right things seemed when he was curled up in Tookie's lap, how her lap was his world, and how his life was shit now that she was dead.

It's nearly five when he returns Nadine's call. The garage has emptied out, but he is still there, cleaning, watching the small black-and-white TV in his dingy waiting room.

"Afraid I've got too much work tonight to have your folks over," he says.

"Another time, I guess. I'll call them."

"I'll see you when I get off."

"Kiss, kiss," she says into the phone.

"The baby okay?"

"Yes," she says. "Kiss, kiss," she repeats.

"Hug, hug," Kevin says. "We'll talk when I get home."

When he gets off the phone, he thinks of his mother and father. He thinks of teasing his sister when they were young—burying her Barbie dolls and stepping through her playhouses. He thinks of the girl he's not sure he has, and he thinks of the child that Nadine is carrying. He daydreams of himself and a mother and child. This time he's not even sure if the baby that comes to him is Ina's or Nadine's. The faceless woman he conjures by his side is smiling. Her head leans back into the sun, but he still can't see her. He's not sure it's Nadine at all, but as clear as if he were watching a movie, he sees his arm crooked around a woman, and she is his wife. A baby is leaning sleepily into her. He tries hard to make Nadine fit into the body of this pretend wife, but he cannot make it so.

He eats a MoonPie from the snack machine and swallows it down with a little bottle of Coke filled with peanuts. He paces back and forth across the floor, each foot sticky with cedar shavings and oil, his mind full of the woman and the little girl. He stands in the waiting room of the garage watching the black-and-white TV until exactly seven o'clock. Maybe he should talk to his father about this. He finishes off his last sip of pop, throws it into the garbage can, then drags his aching, tired body toward home.

1995

A Bird in the Darkness.
A Cluster of Lonely Stars.

Mona

The shadowy figure that slips behind the curtain now looks a bit thinned out, a little slow moving, not the mother that Mona Clark remembers. The face that she remembers is stern and unrelenting, square-jawed and thick. Her mother, the formidable Francine Clark, always sat with her back to the door at a green kitchen table, under the glowing light of one ceiling bulb with a string and chain attached. The back door was open. She hummed while they ate supper. She swatted candle flies and mosquitoes away as they flew toward the light. The kitchen always smelled of bleach.

Though overgrown shrubs shroud the house now and the saggy roof shows years of neglect, back then it wasn't so bad. Francine liked Mona to dress for dinner. So even when she was wearing something perfectly fine, something she had played in all day, Francine still made her go take another bath and put on clean clothes before she could eat. Francine dresses modestly, a simple buttoned-up dress with a cinched waist—where there is an ample stomach and no waistline—and pleats all around it, the buttons secured up to her neck even in the heat of summer.

As a child, Mona watched the lightning bugs dance on

the window screens. She sat at the kitchen table, said grace. They ate supper, as they did every night, in silence. Francine sighed, ignored the sweat beading down the sides of her neck. Her freshly pressed hair coiled and twisted, and the seams under her arms turned dark with sweat. Francine nibbled at her pot roast and gravy, cutting each small piece of meat with her knife, and nodding at Mona to do the same. There was a feast before them, as there was every night—corn, new potatoes boiled in butter and milk, green beans, cornbread, cherry pie. Francine prepared supper as if she was cooking for six. A candle fly lit on the string above their heads, a gnat buzzed at Mona's ear.

Unlike the rowdy Goodes, they were always alone. All those faces around the table, all that sweet noise of family. Mr. Brown's hand always gently at Miss Lucy's back or resting on her knee.

"Mama, was you ever in love?"

While she waited for her mother to answer, Mona excused herself and scraped her plate off into the wastebasket, then went to the door and looked out over the ridge behind their house. She lay her head on the doorframe and breathed in the hills.

Francine corrected her, "Mother, were you ever in love?" but didn't address the question. "I've taught you to speak, Mona Clark. You sound just like one of them country heathens. Close that door, you're letting insects in."

A bird called out in the darkness beyond the heaviness of the humid night. There was a certain smell to all of this—the pines, the dirt, the night itself. Mona closed the door, but stayed there looking out with her nose pressed against the screen.

"God is love, Mona," Francine said. She stood to scrape off her own plate and began to wash the dishes.

The night air fell down around Mona. The blackness went on forever out there. She heard the familiarity of things moving around in the night. Above the house was a moon, a silver bowl dipping into a navy sky. She focused on a cluster of stars, closed her eyes, and prayed: *Dear God, please let me love. Please don't let me curl up and die like a bug. Please, God, send me somebody to love.*

Mona felt her mother watching.

Francine said, "Did I ever tell you it snowed on the night you were born?" and looked off into the dark, as if she was floating somewhere inside the memory itself.

Sitting in her car now, Mona thinks about her mother's stern face, the weight of misery she carries around. All those years with limestone where your back should be would break any woman down, even one the size of Francine Clark.

She takes the house in one more time: the shrubs, the siding, she even thinks she sees a cat, one of Mr. Sugar Britches's kittens maybe. And finally, when her mother's image doesn't return to the window, she just holds Francine in her imagination, places her in her favorite chair, sipping tea and reading the Bible. She tries to hold this thought while she sits in the car, this old idea of her mother, but it floats out, floats back to its long-gone resting place.

In three hours, Mona will be back in the comfort of her own apartment in the city, but now, despite her resistance, her Volvo turns off US-150 back into town, down Main Street to the outskirts where the two-lane narrows into a one-lane. She slows down by the church and again when she reaches her mother's house. She pulls the car off the road and parks. She removes her heels and places them in the passenger's seat, places her silver earrings in the small compartment below the ashtray, and sits in the car until she sees a glimpse of her mother at the window. She'd like to have thought she could determine from this distance if her mother's diabetes is any better, if her cataracts have healed, how her failing kidneys are functioning. Each time she does this, she wishes later that she'd just gone up to the formidable Francine Clark's front door and knocked, said "Mama, I'm home," but she never does. She is not that kind of daughter.

Little Fish.

Lucy

"Mama gone, Granny gone, roots still here."

Lucy mutters this to herself.

House is empty.

Lucy points at her feet.

Where her veins should be, she feels the squash vines growing up from her toes clean up to her head and up through the place where her heart should be. She closes her eyes to make sure they don't drive her blind, but she knows she can't see as well as she used to. Can't breathe as well either. She pinches her nostrils together then lets them loose. Remembers.

Looking out into the yard, she sees Joe bent over the lawnmower, emptying out its guts. From the window, balls of grass look like animals gathered around Joe's feet. The mower moves forward again, and Joe looks back at the work he's done, watching the smooth path forming behind him where the tall grass was. He goes forward looking back, circling from outside to middle.

Over the whir of the mower, Lucy yells through the screen and waves her hand for him to come to her until he sees her there.

He turns to her, mouths "Love you, Lucy," and waves.

"Want a sandwich?" she yells out to him, and holds up a loaf of bread to indicate what she means.

He nods his head, yes. The cooking, cleaning part of her is all he recognizes now, all she recognizes of herself. It's all that's inside her left to give.

In the kitchen, once alive with the banging of pots, Lucy slices bologna onto bread in the unbearable hush of the house. After she pours tea, she shuts her eyes, shakes kitchen ghosts out of her head, puts away mayonnaise.

Like ions of lightning in the dark, memories show themselves, then slip away. She looks down at her hands, which she thinks look just like her mother's. Lucy's fingers seem to be swimming away from her into Tookie's hands, until she closes them into fists.

She peeps around the corner, back into the living room, half expecting to see Minnie Mae or Tookie on the couch. That children's footsteps upstairs? But of course they have all vanished, only dust here and that God-awful emptiness, cruel as death.

Kee Kee and Yolanda gone.

Everything gone.

She peers back out into the yard and sees Joe shooing a cat from the flower bed and gathering the little green mounds into a large plastic bag. The yard is alive with the buzzing and chirping that had been drowned out by the mower. She sits down on the couch and hollers "Dinner!" until the screen door clacks against the jamb. Joe brings a breeze in with him. For a second she thinks she feels like smiling.

Joe sits beside her on the couch, clicks on the television, and begins eating his sandwich. She smells work on him—grease and sweat—and leans her head on his shoulder. This, she thinks, this is what she was put on this earth to do.

"What's for supper?"

"Whiting, grits, shelly beans."

"Need help?"

"Don't need no help."

Joe rests his hand on her knee, eases his tired self up, kisses her forehead, and heads toward the tub. His Lucy. When he gets done taking a bath, he will sit down with her, eat their dinner, and talk about the children or a TV show. She'll want to talk about her mother and grandmother too much, and he'll look at her and say, "Aww, Lucy, them old women did the best they could." Lucy—looking off in the distance somewhere, watching night slipping into the window—knows this, of course. She knows the hearts of the Goode women were filled with best intentions. She knows the difference between good love and bad love. Joe reminds her of this every time.

Lucy goes out onto the porch. She sits down on the steps and pulls a cigarette from her apron pocket. She lights it and blows smoke up toward the sky. She never smoked before, but now she finds it a comfort. Somehow the rings of smoke carry bad memories up toward heaven. Evening is navy blue over the knobs, everything turning dark in the wake of God's shadow.

Her grammar school classmate Rose Helligree whispered to her once, pointing to a man with white hair and skin the color of hedge apple bark, "My mama said that's your daddy." After that, she studied Bruce Harrison, the concave ridge that ran along his cheekbone, and his three beautiful daughters. The Harrison family looked odd because Mr. Bruce was such an old man. But Lucy admired the way he held his daughters' hands when they were walking to the store or to church. Though she never said a word to Mr. Bruce or his daughters, she secretly followed him from the hardware store, the post office, the insurance office, trying to find her own pigeon-toed gait in his walk.

For years she dreamed of drowning, and it was Bruce Harrison who would reach in and lift her from the water as though she were something precious.

So many years ago, in a childhood as filmy as milk, she and Tookie were at the dime store buying fabric for a school dress, when she heard her mother suck in air through her teeth as though she had just received either good news or bad. When she turned, she saw Bruce Harrison and his wife, Miss Katie.

"Nora Jean," he said, nodding at Tookie.

He bent down to Lucy and patted her head like he was petting a dog. "Little Fish," he said to her. He winked and kept walking, with his arm gently resting on Miss Katie's waist.

Tookie left behind the three yards of cotton they needed and rushed out of the store. Lucy remembers her mother standing against the big glass windows outside the store, gathering her breath without speaking. Then she smiled at her and took her hand, and they walked on home. That afternoon, the hills were orangey-ripe with fall.

At Tookie's funeral all those years later, Lucy saw Bruce Harrison in the side vestibule of the church, peering toward her mother's casket from where he stood, his hands stuffed deep in his gray trouser pockets. She saw him flinch when she called out for her mama, his face bunched up like he had a pain somewhere. She would have sworn that's what she saw.

Her grandfather had been there when she was little, before he died, but she was always thinking toward her daddy, whoever he was. Always wondered if Rose Helligree and her mama knew what they were talking about.

Joe walks out onto the porch and sits along the railing, his legs kicking over the side like a boy.

"You need to stop all this smoking, Lucy."

"Calms my nerves."

He looks down at the ground between his legs.

"Did I ever tell you about that time Mama beat me?" she begins.

Still in her mind voices rise up, voices of women telling their own stories, even when she tries to speak out loud over those kitchen ghosts in her head.

Mama gone. Granny gone. Roots still here.

She rubs her arms against the squash vines growing through her elbows down to her finger tips.

"Yes," Joe says, though he knows it's her mother's, Tookie's story that has buoyed up to the surface of her mind. He looks at her as if he's ready to hear it all again, and then suddenly she changes her mind.

"Guess I'd better see if the fish is thawed out."

It has been a month since Joe brought her home from Eastern State. They said she seemed depressed, that was all. Doctor looked at Joe over his glasses and said, "Mr. Brown, I think she'll be fine. Won't you, Mrs. Brown?" He patted Lucy on her shoulder. "This will help," he said. Then pressed the small square of the prescription into Joe's hand.

"You alright?"

"I'm fine, Joe."

She's always wanted Joe to herself. But now that it is just the two of them, she realizes that all she wants is to look at her real daddy just once. And Joe has been a fine replacement until now. Now that voices are whirring through her head and ghosts are appearing in every corner. Sometimes Yolanda comes to her. Not like she is now, full grown, but a baby Yolanda, squalling like she did back then. A scrawny, wiggling thing. No matter how much she tries to erase it from her mind, the picture replays again and again: her forefinger and thumb on that child's nose. Only thing that makes it stop is pinching her own. That baby that comes to her seems to be mocking her when she floats into the room and makes her see her own fingers there, pinching and releasing until it takes her own breath and she has to say to herself, "Breathe, breathe."

When she walks back through the house, the kitchen ghosts are back and she lets them be. Whiting are tremendous in the sink, larger than she remembers. Their bulging eyes stare up at her. Those fingers come back to her again—pinching and pinching, cutting off every bit of wind she has. She swears she hears a baby laugh.

Lucy was eight. The minnows scattered and the water turned a hazy brown as she kicked gravel under her bare feet. She waded into water up to her waist. Her dress billowed out like a hoopskirt.

Minnie Mae was telling her for the fourth time not to go out too far, but then her foot caught a rock covered with algae and she slipped. Her head bobbed up above the water to see her mother there on the bank, her feet frozen to the shore, before she sank once more into the clear waters of Mission Creek. It was Mama Minnie who jumped in to save her. Tookie, who was afraid to move, remained on the creek bank, her blue scarf blowing in the wind, her hand clasped over her mouth.

People around here called Lucy "Little Fish" back then.

Sun is a peach outside the window, grass all calmed down. A bird pecks away at something where one of Joe's grass animals was. She takes up the butcher knife. The butcher knife, her mother's mother's knife. The blade still sharp enough to cut paper. The blade catches the light coming through the windowpane and she slices. When she slices through her wrist, she is reminded of cutting through chicken bone and gristle. There is a certain sound that bone and flesh being sliced makes, something new, but oddly familiar. Familiar as her own two hands, like a raw chicken being cut through.

The Kitchen Ghosts.

Joe

The house feels three-legged to Joe now that Lucy's gone. In her last days she was smoking up a storm and seeing ghosts with that scared, sad look on her face. He could fix a car, fix a broken gasket, an ax handle, anything with a motor. Folks always asking him to fix this and that. And though he had always thought there was nothing he couldn't fix, Joe was helpless against those things that twisted Lucy's mind.

At five in the morning, he goes out to his pickup. The dew is still fresh on the windshield, and an early-morning spiderweb catches him in the face. He places three potted flowers on the passenger's seat and places a hoe and a metal bucket in the truck bed.

It's the day after the funeral. The sky is brightening up, but the sun still shows itself as a muted red ball on the horizon. The trees on the knob are black silhouettes, as though the sun has charred them.

With everything quiet, Joe fights the urge to turn on the radio. He likes the silence, and the reception probably wouldn't last the whole drive anyway. When he crosses Mission Creek Bridge and heads out farther into the country, he hears dogs barking from backyards. He's never owned a dog, never let his children have one. Ain't right to have animals chained to a stake or caged up.

As the sun rises, everything that looked dead changes into shades of green and brown. He drives as slow as the tourists that are starting to swarm downtown. Most of them are crowding into The Depot Restaurant. It used to be the old Greyhound bus station. Now it has the long-front-porch feel of a Cracker Barrel, but with a tin roof and huge wooden boxes of bright red geraniums. The tourists cram inside it to look at the trinkets—mostly cheap replicas of things found over at the Opulence Museum. They flock to the postcards, the stationery, and the old-fashioned toys—spinning tops and real wooden checkers and metal jacks and such—but they come back for Callie Sumner's collards and her fried chicken, and the Formica kitchen tables covered in gingham tablecloths, old-fashioned salt and pepper shakers, and Mason jars of sweet iced tea. This kind of foolishness, trying to grab so tightly to something that used to be, makes Joe laugh, but mostly he wishes these tourists would find somewhere else to go. He has become skeptical of city folks, though he was once one of them himself. Now he belongs here. He is more a Goode than a Brown. He is sure of that now.

Farmers, who've most likely been up before daylight, throw up their hands at him and he nods back. There are not as many black farmers out here as there used to be. Most of them either passed away or left the country for work in the city years ago. And not many of the children ever moved back after they went off to college. He sees the farmers along the way on tractors, with hoes or rakes in their hands. The dairy farmers with their buckets. Otis Turner, cleaning out a pig stall. All that work being done makes him think about all the Weed Eaters and lawnmowers in his shed that need mending. Mrs.

MacAfee has asked him to come by and look at her dishwasher, and he has a chisel plough in the driveway that a man from Bracktown wants him to look at.

When he reaches the entrance of the homeplace, he finds it covered with weeds. He knows that the Goode place is owned by someone else—city white folks he figures—but no matter. This isn't the first time he's been out here since the sale. Every so often he comes just to sit in his truck and think. Sometimes he takes pleasure in watching birds perched in the trees, feeding their young.

He brought Lucy with him once, hoping the fresh air would do her some good. She sat right down in the garden and got eaten up by chiggers. Seemed she had divorced herself from this land long before, back when Yolanda was born out in the squash patch. He remembers the night she refused to nurse the baby, and how the smell of women's blood and sour milk took up the entire room. He remembers the rain ping-pinging on the window, how much he loved Lucy. He could have never left her side, no matter how crazy she was—least folks thought she was crazy; he's not sure even now; could have been some kind of sign from God for all he knows. He remembers how quiet everything was after she calmed down and the women forced her to feed the baby, how even with the cloudy night he could see the outline of the trees out the window. Remembers how much he loved her then and how he's loved her all these years since.

The new owners seem to have abandoned the place. No sign that the grounds have been maintained. Miss Minnie Mae prided herself in keeping it cut and kempt. Always hired a couple of the farmers down the road to bush hog it at the turn of spring and then keep it mowed all summer.

Though it's falling down even more now, he can still see the chimney of the old house; rotting lumber where the well used to be; the overturned smokehouse. He could easily walk it with his eyes closed now after all these years. He knows it foot by foot. He wishes he had come up with the money June and Butter wanted for it when they sold it to the white man.

Joe removes pots from the truck and sits them on the ground, then takes the hoe and water bucket from the truck bed.

He's got some age on him now, but his stride is still good. He carries the first pot out to a spot just beyond the well, facing the hills. The morning is brisk, and he feels the chill across his cheeks.

He takes up the hoe and digs, plants the first bush, and as he pours water he closes his eyes and says, "Minnie Mae Goode, wife of Henry Goode. A fine woman, an old-time woman. Amen."

He plants the second bush where he thinks daffodils used to grow up near the house. "Nora Jean Goode, *Tookie* they called her. Woman had a hard life, but she loved us every one. Amen."

He then goes to the garden spot, which is easy to find because onions have grown wild and are sprouting all over. He can't help but marvel, like he does every time he comes here, that Yolanda was born in this garden. He digs the hole, plants the rose bush and says, "For my beloved Lucy. Mother of my children. My life. Amen." His voice box chokes up and the words come out weaker than he intended. "Amen, Amen, Amen," he says, and then stands back and looks at the fine job he's done.

He stands looking around the place, thinking about Lucy's last days and how she kept on talking about ghosts. She'd been going on about her mother, her grandmother, her great-grandmother. "Lucy, them old women did the best they could," he told her.

Kitchen ghosts, she'd called them. Kept saying, "Mama gone. Granny gone. Roots still here." For the life of him he still doesn't know what she meant. Must've been her mind talking. Them pills didn't do any good. And then Yolanda with those spells, those *panic attacks* as she calls them. He wonders if he might have brought this on his family somehow. He can't help but think that if he'd tried hard enough he could have fixed it—like a sputtering engine or a battery gone bad.

He hangs his head and looks at the grass. Flowers are beginning to bud, their little heads straining toward the light from the soil. He could stay here a week and no one would find him. But the children would worry. He thinks of Yolanda and Kee Kee riding along the back roads in search of him, grieving again. He can't bear thoughts of them losing someone else. He is all they have now. He puts his hands in his pockets and kicks at a beetle. He wonders if there are any copperheads thawing out.

Behind him he hears an engine, and he knows it's a Mack truck before he turns around. If he listens closely, Joe is sure he can identify the exact model. He turns around, and a man with a ruddy face and a red flannel shirt steps from the cab. He is unshaven, and Joe notices his lips are chapped, like he is in need of water.

"You got reason to be here?"

"This was my family's land. Just paying respects."

The man says, "Well get it done, cause we're digging out a pond out here."

The Goodes were never his blood family, but he's found his place among them, and would fight to the death for any Goode, alive or dead.

"Ain't never been no pond here," Joe says. "Used to be a . . ."

"Old man, you best get going."

The man wipes sweat from his forehead and looks at his watch.

Joe sees a hummingbird on the honeysuckle vines along the fence row and stands there watching it. He closes his eyes against finding Lucy on the kitchen floor, and how there was nothing he could do. Nothing no doctor could do either. When he tried to sleep last night, that image kept popping into his head, and he woke up in a cold sweat. He missed her, felt like a man with his insides scooped out.

"I'm going," Joe says.

He walks slowly toward his pickup.

"Get on with it then. We've got a day's work at least."

The truck revs up and heads for the center of the property, and two men roll off a Caterpillar. Joe stands and watches the men doing their work. He kneels down in the dirt, whispers every Goode name he has ever heard spoken, and pours the remaining water in the bucket onto the ground.

He thinks of Lucy when they first married, and how her mother and grandmother told stories up into the night before he and Lucy took to their marriage bed. His initiation, he thinks now. He remembers how wide they opened their arms to him, and how quickly they took him for their own. He shifts the weight of his hips to try and keep his right knee from flaring up again. Lately he has been plagued by bursitis.

He knows that he should get in his pickup and move on back toward home, but he stays there watching as they dig down into the dirt to make way for this pond. He's sure the children are back at the house by now, wondering where he is. The women have made casseroles and pies and are now standing on the porch, waiting to soothe him in his mourning time. His friends have gathered with their pints. They will wait for the women to leave before they get down to real business with that whiskey. He knows there will be gossip about the way Lucy crossed over, but he is past the age to care.

He stands there now, invisible to the working men. Stands while the hole in the earth widens, sees the land devoured by the machine and the shovels. He is sure that if he lays his head on the ground he will hear the voices of the Goode clan bringing in the day with a dirge.

When he leaves the homeplace it is well past noon. He rides back toward his house, convinced that all that's left there are those things out back that need fixing. After the children and the grandchildren and the church women and his friends have left, he will be alone for the second night in more years than he can remember.

And yet, a week from now, though he will still be filled with a deep sorrow, Joe will roar with laughter. John Turner, one of the farmers, will walk into Sam Eaton's little store, where workers come to jabber and whittle.

"Joe," he'll say. "You hear what happened?"

Every man in the store will stop to hear the story. They'll hover over their hog's head cheese and bologna sandwiches wrapped in butcher paper. They'll stop gulping down their little Coca-Colas filled with peanuts to listen.

"Hoot told me that them men that bought up Miss Minnie's place was just a digging on that pond. They dug and dug off and on all week but wasn't quite finished, so they left their bulldozer parked there up on the side there. Up by that bank."

All the men will shake their heads. They will all know just the spot.

"Right up there. You know where that little hill next to the smokehouse dips down a little."

"Yeah," Joe will say.

"Well if it don't beat the devil but them old boys left that Caterpillar in that spot where some of them old-time people had found that underground spring years ago."

The men will nod knowingly in unison.

"They say this old man had witched that well there. But anyway, on Saturday it come the awfulest rain you ever did see . . ."

The men will lean in close because Turner's always been a fine storyteller. They'll be quiet as children, restless for the end. Turner'll stop and chuckle a bit and make them wait for what comes next.

"When them old boys come back on Monday all they could see is the tip top of the seat of that dozer. Said the man that bought the place had to pay double to have somebody come out there and pull that dozer out before they could start up again. We all been laughing about it out yonder since."

Turner will slap his thigh, then slap Joe on the back.

"Miss Minnie's people done come back and gave them folks a piece of their minds. I wouldn't be a bit surprised if it wuddn't Miss Minnie herself leading them all to flood that dozer out."

All the men will laugh, but it will be Joe Brown who will laugh the loudest and the longest, because deep down he will know it to be true. Miss Minnie and Tookie and even his sweet Lucy, all them women who held up the world were out there that day working that dozer—Tookie and Lucy shifting the gears, pulling it first up and back, easy as baking a pie. Miss Minnie looking up at them with her hands on her hips, telling them to go this way or that, careful of the trees.

Joe Brown will look out the store window and watch the sun slide in like a stream of butter. He'll notice the limbs on the birch tree out there in Sam Eaton's yard, fresh with green buds. Then he'll see the three birds up high in the tree, and he'll clap his hands and laugh again, knowing those three women are there with him now too. Still.

Acknowledgments

I am tremendously grateful for my agent, Erin Cox, for her unrelenting critical attention and support, and for her belief in this book from the beginning.

Thank you, Ron Davis, for your unyielding commitment, for loving me, for shepherding our child, the Wild Fig Bookstore, and for everything else.

I am thankful for the fortitude of my literary accomplices: Nikky Finney, Jan Isenhour, Sue Bonner, Robin Lippincott, Connie May Fowler, and Maurice Manning. Thank you for your advice, motivation, and close reading. I also owe a great deal to other members of my writing circle who have provided years of emotional support: Rebecca Gayle Howell, Tayari Jones, Honoree Fanonne Jeffers, Chris Holbrook, and the Affrilachian Poets.

Thank you to AJ Verdelle, whose keen eye and writer's sense showed me how to write again, and then how to rewrite for the highest effect.

I owe a great deal to my entire family at Spalding University's low-residency MFA in Writing Program, especially Sena Jeter Naslund, Neela Vaswani, Silas House, and Jody Lisberger.

Thank you, Kentucky Arts Council and the Kentucky Foundation for Women, for your presence and support for my work and the works of other writer women.

Acknowledgments

A special thanks to my students, who inspire and excite me about words time and time again.

Debra, Darlene, and Trish—I couldn't ask for better sisters. We are all birds together.

Lastly, I want to thank my children, Gerald Wilkinson, Delainia Wilkinson, Elainia Wilkinson, Journey Davis, and Isaac Davis. I love you guys. You will always have home and heart with me.

Kentucky Voices

Miss America Kissed Caleb: Stories
Billy C. Clark

New Covenant Bound
T. Crunk

Next Door to the Dead: Poems
Kathleen Driskell

The Total Light Process: New and Selected Poems
James Baker Hall

Driving with the Dead: Poems
Jane Hicks

Upheaval: Stories
Chris Holbrook

Appalachian Elegy: Poetry and Place
bell hooks

Crossing the River: A Novel
Fenton Johnson

The Man Who Loved Birds: A Novel
Fenton Johnson

Scissors, Paper, Rock: A Novel
Fenton Johnson

Many-Storied House: Poems
George Ella Lyon